ALSO BY YOKO OGAWA

The Diving Pool

YOKO OGAWA

The Housekeeper and the Professor

TRANSLATED FROM THE JAPANESE BY
Stephen Snyder

VINTAGE BOOKS
London

Published by Vintage 2010

6 8 10 9 7

First published in Japan by Shinchosha Co., Ltd. as
Hakase no Aishita Suushiki in 2003.

First published in Great Britain in 2009 by
Harvill Secker

Vintage
Random House, 20 Vauxhall Bridge Road,
London SW1V 2SA

www.vintage-books.co.uk

Addresses for companies within The Random House Group Limited
can be found at: www.randomhouse.co.uk/offices.htm

The Random House Group Limited Reg. No. 954009

A CIP catalogue record for this book
is available from the British Library

ISBN 9780099521341

The Random House Group Limited supports The Forest
Stewardship Council (FSC), the leading international forest
certification organisation. All our titles that are printed on
Greenpeace approved FSC certified paper carry the FSC logo.
Our paper procurement policy can be found at:
www.randomhouse.co.uk/environment

Mixed Sources
Product group from well-managed
forests and other controlled sources
www.fsc.org Cert no. TT-COC-002139
© 1996 Forest Stewardship Council

Printed and bound in Great Britain by
CPI Bookmarque, Croydon CR0 4TD

The

Housekeeper

and the

Professor

1

We called him the Professor. And he called my son Root, because, he said, the flat top of his head reminded him of the square root sign.

"There's a fine brain in there," the Professor said, mussing my son's hair. Root, who wore a cap to avoid being teased by his friends, gave a wary shrug. "With this one little sign we can come to know an infinite range of numbers, even those we can't see." He traced the symbol in the thick layer of dust on his desk.

• • • •

Of all the countless things my son and I learned from the Professor, the meaning of the square root was among the most important. No doubt he would have been bothered by my use of the word *countless*—too sloppy, for he believed that the very origins of the universe could be explained in the exact language of numbers—but I don't know how else to put it. He taught us about enormous prime numbers with more than a hundred thousand places, and the largest number of all, which was used in mathematical proofs and was in the *Guinness Book of Records,* and about the idea of something beyond infinity. As interesting as all this was, it could never match the experience of simply spending time with the Professor. I remember when he taught us about the spell cast by placing numbers under this square root sign. It was a rainy evening in early April. My son's schoolbag lay abandoned on the rug. The light in the Professor's study was dim. Outside the window, the blossoms on the apricot tree were heavy with rain.

The Professor never really seemed to care whether we figured out the right answer to a problem. He preferred our wild, desperate guesses to silence, and he was even more delighted when those guesses led to new problems that took us beyond the original one. He had a special feeling for what he called the "correct miscalculation," for he believed that mistakes were often as revealing as the right answers. This gave us confidence even when our best efforts came to nothing.

"Then what happens if you take the square root of negative one?" he asked.

"So you'd need to get –1 by multiplying a number by itself?"

2

Root asked. He had just learned fractions at school, and it had taken a half-hour lecture from the Professor to convince him that numbers *less* than zero even existed, so this was quite a leap. We tried picturing the square root of negative one in our heads: $\sqrt{-1}$. The square root of 100 is 10; the square root of 16 is 4; the square root of 1 is 1. So the square root of -1 is . . .

He didn't press us. On the contrary, he fondly studied our expressions as we mulled over the problem.

"There is no such number," I said at last, sounding rather tentative.

"Yes, there is," he said, pointing at his chest. "It's in here. It's the most discreet sort of number, so it never comes out where it can be seen. But it's here." We fell silent for a moment, trying to picture the square root of minus one in some distant, unknown place. The only sound was the rain falling outside the window. My son ran his hand over his head, as if to confirm the shape of the square root symbol.

But the Professor didn't always insist on being the teacher. He had enormous respect for matters about which he had no knowledge, and he was as humble in such cases as the square root of negative one itself. Whenever he needed my help, he would interrupt me in the most polite way. Even the simplest request—that I help him set the timer on the toaster, for example—always began with "I'm terribly sorry to bother you, but . . ." Once I'd set the dial, he would sit peering in as the toast browned. He was as fascinated by the toast as he was by the mathematical proofs we did together, as if the truth of the toaster were no different from that of the Pythagorean theorem.

• • • •

It was March of 1992 when the Akebono Housekeeping Agency first sent me to work for the Professor. At the time, I was the youngest woman registered with the agency, which served a small city on the Inland Sea, although I already had more than ten years of experience. I managed to get along with all sorts of employers, and even when I cleaned for the most difficult clients, the ones no other housekeeper would touch, I never complained. I prided myself on being a true professional.

In the Professor's case, it only took a glance at his client card to know that he might be trouble. A blue star was stamped on the back of the card each time a housekeeper had to be replaced, and there were already nine stars on the Professor's card, a record during my years with the agency.

When I went for my interview, I was greeted by a slender, elegant old woman with dyed brown hair swept up in a bun. She wore a knit dress and walked with a cane.

"You will be taking care of my brother-in-law," she said. I tried to imagine why she would be responsible for her husband's brother. "None of the others have lasted long," she continued. "Which has been a terrible inconvenience for me and for my brother-in-law. We have to start again every time a new housekeeper comes. . . . The job isn't complicated. You would come Monday through Friday at 11:00 A.M., fix him lunch, clean the house, do the shopping, make dinner, and leave at 7:00 P.M. That's the extent of it."

There was something hesitant about the way she said the words *brother-in-law*. Her tone was polite enough, but her left hand nervously fingered her cane. Her eyes avoided mine, but occasionally I caught her casting a wary glance in my direction.

"The details are in the contract I signed with the agency. I'm

4

simply looking for someone who can help him live a normal life, like anyone else."

"Is your brother-in-law here?" I asked. She pointed with the cane to a cottage at the back of the garden behind the house. A red slate roof rose above a neatly pruned hedge of scarlet hawthorn.

"I must ask you not to come and go between the main house and the cottage. Your job is to care for my brother-in-law, and the cottage has a separate entrance on the north side of the property. I would prefer that you resolve any difficulties without consulting me. That's the one rule I ask you to respect." She gave a little tap with her cane.

I was used to absurd demands from my employers—that I wear a different color ribbon in my hair every day; that the water for tea be precisely 165 degrees; that I recite a little prayer every evening when Venus rose in the night sky—so the old woman's request struck me as relatively straightforward.

"Could I meet your brother-in-law now?" I asked.

"That won't be necessary." She refused so flatly that I thought I had offended her. "If you met him today, he wouldn't remember you tomorrow."

"I'm sorry, I don't understand."

"He has difficulties with his memory," she said. "He's not senile; his brain works well, but about seventeen years ago he hit his head in an automobile accident. Since then, he has been unable to remember anything new. His memory stops in 1975. He can remember a theorem he developed thirty years ago, but he has no idea what he ate for dinner last night. In the simplest terms, it's as if he has a single, eighty-minute videotape inside his head, and when he records anything new, he has to record over the existing memories. His memory lasts precisely eighty minutes—no more and no less." Perhaps because she had repeated this explanation so many times in the past, the old woman ran through it without pause, and with almost no sign of emotion.

How exactly does a man live with only eighty minutes of memory? I had cared for ailing clients on more than one occasion in the past, but none of that experience would be useful here. I could just picture a tenth blue star on the Professor's card.

From the main house, the cottage appeared deserted. An old-fashioned garden door was set into the hawthorn hedge, but it was secured by a rusty lock that was covered in bird droppings.

"Well then, I'll expect you to start on Monday," the old woman said, putting an end to the conversation. And that's how I came to work for the Professor.

Compared to the impressive main house, the cottage was modest to the point of being shabby: a small bungalow that seemed to have been built hastily. Trees and shrubs had grown wild around it, and the doorway was deep in shadows. When I tried the doorbell on Monday, it seemed to be broken.

"What's your shoe size?"

This was the Professor's first question, once I had announced myself as the new housekeeper. No bow, no greeting. If there is one ironclad rule in my profession, it's that you always give the employer what he wants; and so I told him.

"Twenty-four centimeters."

"There's a sturdy number," he said. "It's the factorial of four." He folded his arms, closed his eyes, and was silent for a moment.

"What's a 'factorial'?" I asked at last. I felt I should try to find out a bit more, since it seemed to be connected to his interest in my shoe size.

"The product of all the natural numbers from one to four is twenty-four," he said, without opening his eyes. "What's your telephone number?"

He nodded, as if deeply impressed. "That's the total number of primes between one and one hundred million."

It wasn't immediately clear to me why my phone number was so interesting, but his enthusiasm seemed genuine. And he wasn't showing off; he struck me as straightforward and modest. It nearly convinced me that there *was* something special about my phone number, and that I was somehow special for having it.

Soon after I began working for the Professor, I realized that he talked about numbers whenever he was unsure of what to say or do. Numbers were also his way of reaching out to the world. They were safe, a source of comfort.

Every morning, during the entire time I worked for the Professor, we repeated this numerical q and a at the front door. To the Professor, whose memory lasted only eighty minutes, I was always a new housekeeper he was meeting for the first time, and so every morning he was appropriately shy and reserved. He would ask my shoe size or telephone number, or perhaps my zip code, the registration number on my bicycle, or the number of brushstrokes in the characters of my name; and whatever the number, he invariably found some significance in it. Talk of factorials and primes flowed effortlessly, seeming completely natural, never forced.

Later, even after I had learned the meanings of some of these terms, there was still something pleasant about our daily introductions at the door. I found it reassuring to be reminded that my telephone number had some significance (beyond its usual purpose), and the simple sound of the numbers helped me to start the day's work with a positive attitude.

He had once been an expert in number theory at a university. He was sixty-four, but he looked older and somewhat haggard, as though he did not eat properly. He was barely more than five feet tall, and his back was so badly hunched that he seemed even shorter. The wrinkles on his bony neck looked a little grimy, and his wispy, snow-white hair fell in all directions, half-concealing his plump, Buddhalike ears. His voice was feeble and his movements were slow. If you looked closely, though, you could see traces of a face that had once been handsome. There was something in the sharp line of his jaw and his deeply carved features that was still attractive.

Whether he was at home or going out—which he did very rarely—the Professor always wore a suit and tie. His closet held three suits, one for winter, one for summer, and one that could be worn in spring or fall, three neckties, six shirts, and an overcoat. He did not own a sweater or a pair of casual pants. From a housekeeper's point of view, it was the ideal closet.

I suspect that the Professor had no idea there were clothes other than suits. He had no interest in what people wore, and even less in his own appearance. For him it was enough to get up in the morning, open the closet, and put on whichever suit wasn't wrapped in plastic from the cleaners. All three suits were dark and well-worn, much like the Professor himself, and clung to him like a second skin.

But by far the most curious thing about the Professor's appearance was the fact that his suit was covered with innumerable scraps of notepaper, each one attached to him by a tiny binder clip. Every conceivable surface—the collar, cuffs, pockets, hems, belt loops, and buttonholes—was covered with notes, and the binder clips gathered the fabric of his clothing in awkward bunches. The notes were simply scraps of torn paper, some yellowing or crumbling. In order to read them, you had to get close and squint, but it soon became clear that he was compensating for his lack of memory by writing down the things he absolutely had to remember and pinning them where he couldn't lose them—on his body. His odd appearance was as distracting as his questions about my shoe size.

"Come in then," he said. "I have to work, but you just do whatever it is you have to do." And with that he disappeared into his study. As he turned and walked away, the notes made a dry, rustling sound.

From the bits and pieces of information I gleaned from the nine housekeepers who had come before me, it seemed that the old woman in the main house was a widow, and that her husband had been the Professor's older brother. When their parents had died, his brother had taken over the family textile business, had enlarged it considerably, and willingly assumed the cost of educating a brother who was a dozen years younger. In this way, the Professor had been able to pursue his study of mathematics at Cambridge University. But soon after he had received his doctorate and had found a position at a research institute, his brother had died suddenly of acute hepatitis. The widow, who had no children, decided to close down the factory, put up an apartment building on the land, and live off the rents she collected.

In the years that followed, the Professor and his sister-in-law had settled peacefully into their respective lives—until the accident. A truck driver had dozed off and struck the Professor's car head-on. He had suffered irreversible brain damage and had eventually lost his position at the university. He was forty-seven at the time, and since then he'd had no income except the prize money he earned from solving contest problems in the mathematics journals. For seventeen years he had been completely dependent on the widow's charity.

"You have to feel sorry for the old woman," one of the former housekeepers had said. "Having that strange brother-in-law eat through what her husband left her like some parasite." She'd been sent packing after she complained about the Professor's incessant jabbering about numbers.

The inside of the cottage was as cold and uninviting as the outside. There were just two rooms, an eat-in kitchen and a study that doubled as the Professor's bedroom. It was small, and the wretched condition of the place was striking. The furniture was cheap, the wallpaper was discolored, and the floor in the hall creaked miserably. The doorbell wasn't the only thing that didn't work: just about everything in the house was either broken or on its last legs. The little window in the bathroom was cracked, the knob on the kitchen door was falling off, and the radio that sat on top of the dish cupboard made no sound when I tried to turn it on.

The first two weeks were exhausting, since I had no idea what I was supposed to be doing. The work wasn't physically demanding, and yet at the end of each day my muscles were stiff and my whole body felt heavy. It was always a struggle at each new assignment until I adapted to the rhythm of the work, but the adjustment was especially difficult with the Professor. In most cases, I figured out what sort of person I was dealing with from the things they told me to do, or not to do. I determined where to focus my efforts, how to avoid getting into trouble—how to read the demands of the job. But the Professor never gave me instruction of any kind, as though he did not mind what I did.

On that first day, it occurred to me that I should simply follow what the old woman had said, and start by fixing the Professor's lunch. I checked the refrigerator and the kitchen cupboards, but I found nothing edible except for a box of damp oatmeal and some macaroni and cheese that was four years past its expiration date.

I knocked at the study door. There was no answer, so I knocked again. Still no answer. I knew I shouldn't, but I opened the door and spoke to the Professor's back as he sat at his desk.

"I'm sorry to disturb you," I said.

He gave no sign of having heard me. Perhaps he's hard of hearing, or wearing earplugs, I thought. "What would you like for lunch?" I continued. "Are there . . . things you like or dislike? Do you have any food allergies?"

The study smelled of books. Half the windows were covered by bookshelves, and piles of books drifted up the walls. A bed with a worn-out mattress was pressed against one wall. There was a single notebook lying open on the desk, but no computer, and the Professor wasn't holding a pen or pencil. He simply stared at a fixed point off in space.

"If there's nothing particular you want, I'll just make something. But please don't hesitate if there's anything I can get for you."

I happened to glance at some of the notes pinned to his suit: ". . . the failure of the analytic method . . . ," ". . . Hilbert's thirteenth . . . ," ". . . the function of the elliptical curve. . . ." Shuffled in among the fragments of obscure numbers and symbols and words was one scrap that even I could understand. From the stains and bent corners of the paper and the rusted edges of the binder clip, I could tell that this one had been attached to the Professor for a long time: "My memory lasts only eighty minutes," it read.

"I have nothing to say," he said, turning suddenly and speaking in a loud voice. "I'm thinking at the moment. *Thinking.* And to have my thoughts interrupted is like being strangled. Don't you know that barging in here when I'm with my numbers is as rude as interrupting someone in the bathroom?"

I bowed and apologized repeatedly, but I doubt he heard a word of what I said. He had already returned to his fixed point somewhere off in space.

To be shouted at like that on the first day could be a serious problem, and I worried that I might become the tenth star on his file card before I'd even started. I promised myself that I would never disturb him again while he was "thinking."

But the Professor was always thinking. When he came out of the study and sat at the table, when he was gargling in the bathroom, or even when he did his strange stretching exercises, he continued thinking. He ate whatever was set in front of him, mechanically shoveling the food in his mouth and swallowing almost without chewing. He had a distracted, unsteady way of walking. I managed to find the right moment to ask him about things I needed to know—where he kept the wash bucket or how to use the water heater. And I avoided making any unnecessary noise, even breathing too loudly, as I moved about that unfamiliar house, waiting for him to take even a short break from his thinking.

I made a cream stew for dinner, something with vegetables and protein that he could eat with just a spoon—and that he could eat without removing bones or shells. Perhaps it was because he'd lost his parents at such a young age, but he had less than perfect table manners. He never said a word of thanks before he started eating, and he spilled food with almost every bite. I even caught him cleaning his ears with his dirty napkin at the table. He did not complain about my cooking, and he remained silent as he ate. Each time he plunged the spoon into the stew, he looked as if he might lose it in the bowl.

"Would you like some more? I've made plenty." It was careless of me to speak up suddenly like that, to take such a familiar tone, and all I got by way of an answer was a burp. Without so much as a glance in my direction, he got up and disappeared into his study. There was a small pile of carrots at the bottom of his bowl.

At the end of my first day, I noticed a new note on the cuff of his jacket. "The new housekeeper," it said. The words were written in tiny, delicate characters, and above them was a sketch of a woman's face. It looked like the work of a small child—short hair, round cheeks, and a mole next to the mouth—but I knew instantly that it was a portrait of me. I imagined the Professor hurrying to draw this likeness before the memory had vanished. The note was proof of something, that he had interrupted his thinking for my sake.

Over the next few days, I introduced myself by pointing to the note on his cuff. The Professor would be silent for a moment, comparing my face with the picture on his sleeve, trying to recall what the note had meant. At last he would make a little huffing sound and ask me my shoe size and telephone number. But I realized that something dramatic had changed when, at the end of my first week, he came to me with a bundle of papers covered with formulas and numbers, and asked me to send it off to the *Journal of Mathematics*.

"I'm terribly sorry to bother you, but . . ."

His tone was polite, and completely unexpected after the way he had scolded me in his study on my first day. It was the first request he had made of me, and he was no longer "thinking," for the moment.

"It's no trouble at all," I told him. I carefully copied the mysterious foreign address onto the envelope and ran off happily to the post office.

When I returned, the Professor wasn't thinking anymore. He was stretched out in the easy chair by the kitchen window, and as he rested I was finally able to clean the study. I opened the windows and took his quilt and pillow out into the garden to air. And then I ran the vacuum cleaner at full throttle. The room was cluttered and chaotic, but comfortable.

I was not surprised to find balls of hair and moldy Popsicle sticks behind the desk, or a chicken bone resting on top of one of his bookshelves. And yet, the room was filled by a kind of stillness. Not simply an absence of noise, but an accumulation of layers of silence, untouched by fallen hair or mold, silence that the Professor left behind as he wandered through the numbers, silence like a clear lake hidden in the depths of the forest.

But despite its relative comfort, if you had asked me whether it was an interesting room, I would have had to say no. There was not a single object to spark the imagination, no trinkets from the Professor's past, no mysterious photographs or decorations that might have amused a housekeeper.

I attacked the bookshelves with the duster. *Group Theory. Algebraic Number Theory. Studies in Number Theory.* . . . Chevalley,

Hamilton, Turing, Hardy, Baker. . . . So many books and not one I wanted to read. Half of them were in foreign languages, and I couldn't even make out the titles on the spines. A few notebooks were stacked on the desk, along with a scattering of pencil stubs and binder clips. How could he *think* at such a characterless desk? The residue from an eraser was the only evidence of the work that he had done here.

As I wiped away the dust, arranged the notebooks, and gathered up the clips, it occurred to me that a mathematician ought to have some sort of expensive compass you couldn't find in an ordinary stationery shop, or an elaborate slide rule. The seat of the chair was worn down where the Professor sat.

"When is your birthday?"

That evening after dinner, he did not disappear immediately into his study. Though I was busy cleaning up, he seemed to be looking for a topic of conversation.

"February twentieth."

"Is that so?"

The Professor had picked the carrots out of his potato salad and had left them on the plate. I cleared and wiped the table, noticing that he still seemed to spill a great deal, even when he wasn't thinking. It was spring, but still chilly once the sun set, so the oil heater was burning in the corner.

"Do you send a lot of articles to magazines?" I asked.

"I wouldn't call them 'articles.' They're just puzzles for amateur mathematicians. Sometimes there's even a prize. Wealthy men who love mathematics put up the money." He looked down, checking his suit in various places, and his gaze fell on a note clipped to his left pocket. "Oh, I see. I sent a proof to the *Journal of Mathematics* today."

It had been much more than eighty minutes since I'd made my trip to the post office.

"Oh, dear!" I said. "If it's a contest, I should have sent it express mail. If it doesn't get there first, I suppose you don't get the prize."

"No, there was no need to send it express. Of course, it's important to arrive at the correct answer before anyone else, but it's just as important that the proof is elegant."

"I had no idea a proof could be beautiful . . . or ugly."

"Of course it can," he said. Getting up from the table, he came over to the sink where I was washing the dishes and peered at me as he continued. "The truly correct proof is one that strikes a harmonious balance between strength and flexibility. There are plenty of proofs that are technically correct but are messy and inelegant or counterintuitive. But it's not something you can put into words—explaining why a formula is beautiful is like trying to explain why the stars are beautiful."

I stopped washing and nodded, not wanting to interrupt the Professor's first real attempt at conversation.

"Your birthday is February twentieth. Two twenty. Can I show you something? This was a prize I won for my thesis on transcendent number theory when I was at college." He took off his wristwatch and held it up for me to see. It was a stylish foreign brand, quite out of keeping with the Professor's rumpled appearance.

"It's a wonderful prize," I said.

"But can you see the number engraved here?" The inscription on the back of the case read President's Prize No. 284.

"Does that mean that it was the two hundred and eighty-fourth prize awarded?"

"I suppose so, but the interesting part is the number 284 itself.

Take a break from the dishes for a moment and think about these two numbers: 220 and 284. Do they mean anything to you?"

Pulling me by my apron strings, he sat me down at the table and produced a pencil stub from his pocket. On the back of an advertising insert, he wrote the two numbers, separated strangely on the card.

220

                                                            284

"Well, what do you make of them?"

I wiped my hands on my apron, feeling awkward, as the Professor looked at me expectantly. I wanted to respond, but had no idea what sort of answer would please a mathematician. To me, they were just numbers.

"Well . . . ," I stammered. "I suppose you could say they're both three-digit numbers. And that they're fairly similar in size—for example, if I were in the meat section at the supermarket, there'd be very little difference between a package of sausage that weighed 220 grams and one that weighed 284 grams. They're so close that I would just buy the one that was fresher. They seem pretty much the same—they're both in the two hundreds, and they're both even—"

"Good!" he almost shouted, shaking the leather strap of his watch. I didn't know what to say. "It's important to use your intuition. You swoop down on the numbers, like a kingfisher catching the glint of sunlight on the fish's fin." He pulled up a chair, as if wanting to be closer to the numbers. The musty paper smell from the study clung to the Professor.

"You know what a factor is, don't you?"

"I think so. I'm sure I learned about them at some point. . . ."

"For 220 is divisible by 1 and by 220 itself, with nothing leftover. So 1 and 220 are factors of 220. Natural numbers always have 1 and the number itself as factors. But what else can you divide it by?"

"By 2, and 10. . . ."

"Exactly! So let's try writing out the factors of 220 and 284, excluding the numbers themselves. Like this."

```
220 : 1  2  4  5  10  11  20  22  44  55  110
      142  71  4  2  1 : 284
```

The Professor's figures, rounded and slanting slightly to one side, were surrounded by black smears where the pencil had smudged.

"Did you figure out all the factors in your head?" I asked.

"I don't have to calculate them—they just come to me from the same kind of intuition you used. So then, let's move on to the next step," he said, adding symbols to the lists of factors.

```
220 : 1 + 2 + 4 + 5 + 10 + 11 + 20 + 22 + 44 + 55 + 110 =
      =142 + 71 + 4 + 2 + 1 : 284
```

"Add them up," he said. "Take your time. There's no hurry."

He handed me the pencil, and I did the calculation in the space that was left on the advertisement. His tone was kind and full of expectation, and it didn't seem as though he were testing me. On the contrary, he made me feel as though I were on an important mission, that I was the only one who could lead us out of this puzzle and find the correct answer.

I checked my calculations three times to be sure I hadn't made

THE HOUSEKEEPER AND THE PROFESSOR

a mistake. At some point, while we'd been talking, the sun had set and night was falling. From time to time I heard water dripping from the dishes I had left in the sink. The Professor stood close by, watching me.

"There," I said. "I'm done."

$$220 : 1 + 2 + 4 + 5 + 10 + 11 + 20 + 22 + 44 + 55 + 110 = 284$$

$$220 = 142 + 71 + 4 + 2 + 1 : 284$$

"That's right! The sum of the factors of 220 is 284, and the sum of the factors of 284 is 220. They're called 'amicable numbers,' and they're extremely rare. Fermat and Descartes were only able to find one pair each. They're linked to each other by some divine scheme, and how incredible that your birthday and this number on my watch should be just such a pair."

We sat staring at the advertisement for a long time. With my finger I traced the trail of numbers from the ones the Professor had written to the ones I'd added, and they all seemed to flow together, as if we'd been connecting up the constellations in the night sky.

2

That evening, after I'd got home and put my son to bed, I decided to look for "amicable numbers" on my own. I wanted to see whether they were really as rare as the Professor had said, and since it was just a matter of writing out factors and adding them up, I was sure I could do it, even though I'd never graduated from high school.

But I soon realized what I was up against. Following the Professor's suggestion, I tried using my intuition to pick likely pairs, but I had no luck. I stuck to even numbers at first, thinking the factors would be easier to find, and I tried every pair between ten and one hundred. Then I expanded my search to odd numbers, and then to three-digit numbers as well, still to no effect. Far from being amicable, the numbers seemed to turn their backs on each other, and I couldn't find a pair with even the most tenuous connection—let alone this wonderfully intimate one. The Professor was right: my birthday and his watch had overcome great trials and tribulations to meet each other in the vast sea of numbers.

Soon, every inch of the paper was filled with figures. My method was logical, if a little primitive—yet I ended up with nothing to show for all my work.

I did make one small discovery: the sum of the factors of 28 equals 28.

$$28 : 1 + 2 + 4 + 7 + 14 = 28$$

Though I wasn't sure this amounted to anything. None of the other numbers I'd tried were the sum of their own factors, but that didn't mean there weren't more out there. I knew it was an exaggeration to call it a "discovery," but for me it was just that. This one line of numbers stretched across the page as if pulled taut by some mysterious intention.

As I got into bed, I finally glanced at the clock. It had been much more than eighty minutes since we'd had our talk about amicable numbers. By now he'd have forgotten all about our secret, and he'd have no idea where the number 220 had come from. I found it difficult to fall asleep.

From a housekeeper's perspective, working for the Professor was relatively easy: a small house, no visitors or phone calls, and only light meals for one man who had little interest in food. At other jobs, I always had to do as much as possible in a short amount of time; but now I was delighted to have so much time to do a truly thorough job of cleaning, washing, and cooking. I learned to recognize when the Professor was beginning a new contest, and how to avoid disturbing him. I polished the kitchen table to my heart's content with a special varnish and patched the mattress on his bed. I even invented various ways to camouflage the carrots in his dinner.

The one thing about the job that was always a little tricky was understanding how the Professor's memory worked. According to the old woman, he remembered nothing after 1975; but I had no idea what yesterday meant to him or whether he could think ahead to tomorrow, or how much he suffered.

It was clear that he didn't remember me from one day to the next. The note clipped to his sleeve simply informed him that it was not our first meeting, but it could not bring back the memory of the time we had spent together.

When I went out shopping, I tried to return home within an hour and twenty minutes. As befit a mathematician, the device in his brain that measured those eighty minutes was more precise than any clock. If an hour and eighteen minutes had passed from the time I walked out the door to the time I got back, I would receive a friendly welcome; but after an hour and twenty-two minutes, we were back to "What's your shoe size?"

I was always afraid of making some careless remark that might upset him. I nearly bit my tongue once when I started to mention something the newspaper had said about Prime Minister Miyazawa. (For the Professor, the prime minister was still Takeo Miki.) And I felt awful about suggesting that we get a television to watch the summer Olympics in Barcelona. (His last Olympics were in Munich.) Still, the Professor gave no sign that this bothered him. When the conversation veered off in a direction he couldn't follow, he simply waited patiently until it returned to a topic he could handle. But, for his part, he never asked me anything about myself, how long I'd been working as a housekeeper, where I came from, or whether I had a family. Perhaps he was afraid of bothering me by repeating the same question again and again.

The one topic we could discuss without any worry was mathematics. Not that I was enthusiastic about it at first. In school, I had hated math so much that the mere sight of the textbook made me feel ill. But the things the Professor taught me seemed to find their way effortlessly into my brain—not because I was an employee anxious to please her employer but because he was a such a gifted teacher. There was something profound in his love for math. And it helped that he forgot what he'd taught me before, so I was free to repeat the same question until I understood. Things that most people would get the first time around might take me five, or even ten times, but I could go on asking the Professor to explain until I finally got it.

"The person who discovered amicable numbers must have been a genius."

"You might say that: it was Pythagoras, in the sixth century B.C."

"Did they have numbers that long ago?"

"Of course! Did you think they were invented in the nineteenth century? There were numbers before human beings—before the world itself was formed."

We talked about numbers while I worked in the kitchen. The

23

Professor would sit at the kitchen table or relax in the easy chair by the window, while I stirred something on the stove or washed the dishes at the sink.

"Is that so? I'd always thought that human beings invented numbers."

"No, not at all. If that were the case, they wouldn't be so difficult to understand and there'd be no need for mathematicians. No one actually witnessed the first numbers come into being—when we first became aware of them, they'd already been around for a long time."

"And that's why so many smart people try so hard to figure out how they work?"

"Yes, and why human beings seem so foolish and frail compared to whoever or whatever created these numbers." The Professor sat back in his chair and opened one of his journals.

"Well, hunger makes you even more foolish and frail, so we need to feed that brain of yours. Dinner will be ready in a minute." Having finished grating some carrots to mix into his hamburger, I carefully slipped the peelings into the garbage pail. "By the way," I added, "I've been trying to find another pair of amicable numbers besides 220 and 284, but I haven't had any luck."

"The next smallest pair is 1,184 and 1,210."

"Four digits? No wonder I didn't find them. I even had my son help me. I found the factors, and then he added them up."

"You have a son?" The Professor sat up in his chair; his magazine slipped to the floor.

"Yes."

"How old is he?"

"Ten."

"Ten? He's just a little boy!" The Professor's expression had quickly darkened, he was becoming agitated. I stopped mixing the hamburger and waited for what I was sure was coming: a lesson on the significance of the number 10.

"And where is your son now?" he said.

"Well, let's see. He's home from school by now, but he's probably given up on his homework and gone to the park to play baseball with his friends."

" 'Well, let's see'! How can you be so nonchalant? It'll be dark soon!"

I was wrong, there would be no revelations about the number 10, it seemed. In this case, 10 was the age of a small boy, and nothing more.

"It's all right," I said. "He does this every day."

"Every day! You abandon your son every day so you can come here to make hamburgers?"

"I don't abandon him, and it's my job to come here." I wasn't sure why the Professor was so concerned about my son, but I went back to my recipe, adding some pepper and nutmeg.

"Who takes care of him when you're not home? Does your husband come home early from work? Does his grandmother watch him?"

"No, unfortunately there's no husband or grandmother. It's just the two of us."

"So he's at home all alone? He sits and waits for his mother in a dark house while you're here making dinner for a stranger? Making *my* dinner!"

No longer able to control himself, the Professor jumped up from his chair and began circling the table. The notes on his body trembled as he ran his hand nervously through his hair. Dandruff sprinkled on his shoulder. I turned off the soup just as it began to boil.

"You really don't need to worry," I said, trying to sound calm. "We've been doing this since he was much younger. Now that he's ten, he can manage for himself. He has the phone number here, and if he needs help, he knows to ask the landlord downstairs—"

"No, no, no!" The Professor cut me off as he paced around the table. "You should *never* leave a child alone. What if the heater fell over and started a fire? What if he choked on a candy? Who'd be there to help? Oh! I don't want to think about it. Go home right now! You should make dinner for your child. Go home!" He grabbed my arm and tried to pull me toward the door.

"I'll go," I said, "but I just have to make these hamburgers for you."

"Are you going to stand there frying hamburgers while your child could be dying in a fire? Now listen to me: beginning tomorrow you'll bring your son along with you. He can come straight here from school. He can do his homework, and be near his mother. And don't think you can fool me just because I'll forget by tomorrow."

He pulled off the tag that read "the new housekeeper" and fished a pencil from his pocket. Under the portrait, he added the words "and her son, ten years old."

I left that evening—or rather, I was chased out—without having time to wash my hands, let alone clean the kitchen properly. The Professor appeared even angrier than when I had interrupted his thinking. But his anger seemed to hide a deep fear, and I hurried home wondering what I would do if I found the apartment in flames.

Any reticence or wariness I felt for the Professor vanished the moment I saw him with my son, and from that point on I trusted him completely. As I'd promised the evening before, I gave my son a map to the house and told him to come directly from school. It was against agency rules to bring children to the workplace, but there was no denying the Professor.

When my son appeared at the door the next day with his schoolbag on his back, the Professor broke into a wide grin and opened his arms to embrace him. I didn't even have time to point at the line he'd added to his note—"and her son, ten years old." As a mother, it was a joy to see someone so completely embrace my child, and I felt a slight twinge of jealousy that my welcome from the Professor was always much more reserved.

"I'm so glad you've come!" he said, without any of the questions he asked me every morning. Bewildered by the unexpected greeting, my son stiffened, but managed a polite answer. The Professor took off my son's Hanshin Tigers baseball cap and rubbed his head. Then he gave him the nickname before he'd even learned his real one.

"I'm going to call you Root," he said. "The square root sign is a generous symbol, it gives shelter to all the numbers." And he quickly took off the note on his sleeve and made the addition: "The new housekeeper . . . and her son, ten years old, $\sqrt{}$."

At first I made us name tags, thinking that if the Professor weren't the only one with notes clipped to him he might feel less anxious. I told my son to change his school name tag for one I made that read "$\sqrt{}$." The experiment proved less successful than I'd hoped. No matter how much time passed, I was always the young woman who made painfully slow progress with numbers, and my son would be the boy who simply appeared, and was embraced.

My son soon grew accustomed to the Professor's enthusiastic

greeting and even came to enjoy it. He would take off his cap at the door and present the flat top of his head, as if to show how proud he was to be worthy of the name Root. And for his part, the Professor never missed his cue, he mentioned the square root whenever he met my son.

My contract stipulated that I would make dinner for him at six o'clock and leave at seven after finishing the dishes; but the Professor began objecting to this schedule as soon as my son arrived on the scene.

"I won't stand for it! If you have to finish here and then make another meal once you get home, Root won't get his dinner until eight o'clock. That just won't do. It's inefficient; it's illogical. Children should be in bed by eight o'clock. You can't deprive a child of his sleep—that's when he does his growing."

For a mathematician, his argument wasn't very scientific, but I decided to ask the director of the agency if it would be possible to deduct the cost of our dinner from my salary.

The Professor had never before thanked me for my efforts in the kitchen, but his attitude changed when the three of us sat down to dinner together for the first time. His manners were exemplary. He sat up very straight and ate quietly, without spilling so much as a drop of his soup on the table or his napkin—all of which seemed odd, given how terrible his manners had been when it was just the two of us.

"What's the name of your school?" he asked.

"Is your teacher nice?

"How was lunch today?

"What do you want to be when you grow up?"

As he squeezed lemon on his chicken or picked out the carrots from his soup, the Professor would ask Root one question after another, without hesitating, even when the question concerned the past or the future. He was determined to make our dinner hour as peaceful and pleasant as possible. Though Root's answers to his questions were mostly perfunctory, the Professor listened attentively, and it was thanks to his efforts that we ate together without drifting into any awkward silences.

He was not simply humoring a child. Whenever Root would put his elbows on the table or clatter his dishes or commit any other breach of etiquette (all things the Professor had done himself at his earlier solitary meals), the Professor would gently correct him.

"You have to eat more," he said one evening. "A child's job is to grow."

"I'm the shortest one in my class," said Root.

"Don't let that bother you. You're storing up energy, pretty soon you'll have a growth spurt. One of these days, you're going to feel your bones begin to stretch out and grow."

"Did that happen to you?" Root wanted to know.

"No, unfortunately, in my case, all that energy was wasted on other things."

"What other things?"

"On my friends. I had some very close friends, but as it turned out they weren't the sort you could play baseball or kick-the-can with. In fact, playing with them didn't involve moving at all."

"Were your friends sick?"

"Just the opposite. They were big and strong as a rock. But since they lived in my head, I could only play with them there. So I ended up growing a strong brain instead of a strong body."

"I see," said Root. "Your friends were numbers. My mom says you're a great math teacher."

"You're a bright boy. Very bright. That's correct, numbers were my only friends. . . . But that's why you need to get lots of exercise while you're young. Do you understand? And you have to eat everything on your plate, even the things you don't like. And if you're still hungry, you can have anything on my plate, too."

"Thanks!"

Root had never enjoyed dinner as much as he did when we ate with the Professor. He answered the Professor's questions and let him fill his plate to overflowing, and whenever he could, he looked curiously around the room or stole a glance at the notes on the Professor's suit.

Root was a child who had rarely been embraced. When I first saw him in the hospital nursery, I felt something closer to fear than to joy. His eyelids and earlobes and even his feet were still swollen and damp from the amniotic fluid. His eyes were half-closed, but he didn't seem to be asleep. His tiny arms and legs, protruding awkwardly from the oversized gown, flailed from time to time as if in protest at having been left here by mistake.

I was eighteen, ignorant, and alone. My cheeks were sunken from morning sickness that had continued right up to the moment I lay down on the delivery table. My hair stank with sweat, and my pajamas were still stained where my water had broken.

There were fifteen babies in the nursery and he was the only one awake. It was before dawn and the halls were empty except for the women at the nurse's station. His fists had been clenched tight, but at that moment he opened them, and then awkwardly bent them closed again. The small fingernails were dark and discolored with traces of what I assumed was my blood.

"Excuse me," I called, staggering down to the nurse's station. "I'd like to cut my baby's fingernails. He seems to be moving his hands a lot and I'm afraid he'll scratch himself. . . ." Perhaps I was trying to convince myself that I was a good mother.

From the time of my earliest memories, I had no father. My mother had fallen in love with a man she could never marry, and she had raised me by herself. She worked at a reception hall that people hired for weddings. She had started out helping wherever she was needed—bookkeeping, dressing the wedding parties, flower arranging, table coordination—and ended up managing the whole place.

She was a strong woman who hated nothing more than having people think of her daughter as poor and fatherless. Though we were, in fact, poor, she did her best to make us look and feel rich. She asked the women who worked in the dressmaking department to give us scraps of material from which she made all my clothes. She arranged for the organist at the hall to give me piano lessons at a discount. And she brought home the leftover flowers and made pretty arrangements for the apartment.

I suppose I became a housekeeper because I kept house for my mother from the time I was a small child. When I was barely two and not quite potty trained, I would wash out my own panties if I had an accident; and before I was even in elementary school, I was using the knives in the kitchen and cutting up the ingredients to make fried rice. By the time I was ten, I not only took care of the whole apartment, but I was even paying the electric bill and attending meetings of the neighborhood association in my mother's place.

My mother never said a word against my father and always insisted he was a fine man and terribly handsome. He managed a restaurant somewhere, but the specifics were always kept from me. I was given to understand, however, that he was tall, fluent in English, and a connoisseur of opera.

The image I have of my father is that of a statue in a museum. No matter how close I come to him, I can't get his attention, he continues to stare off into the distance without looking down, and he never reaches out his hand to me.

It wasn't until I entered adolescence that it occurred to me how odd it was that the wonderful man my mother described had abandoned us and had never offered even the least bit of economic support. But by that time I had no interest in learning more about him, and I accepted the role of silent accomplice when it came to my mother's illusions.

It was my pregnancy that utterly destroyed those illusions, along with the others she'd carefully stitched together from fabric scraps, piano lessons, and leftover flowers. It happened not long after I'd started my junior year of high school.

The boy was someone I'd met at my after-school job, a college student majoring in electrical engineering. He was a quiet and cultured young man, but he lacked the decency to take responsibility for what had happened. The mysterious knowledge of electricity that had attracted me to him in the first place proved useless, and he became just another careless man who vanished from my world.

Once my pregnancy became obvious, there was nothing I could do to appease my mother's anger, even though we now shared the experience of giving birth to a fatherless child. It was a melodramatic sort of anger. Her feelings seemed to block out my own. I left home in the twenty-second week of my pregnancy and I lost all contact with her.

When I brought my baby home from the hospital, it was to public housing that had been set up for single mothers, and the only person who welcomed us was the woman who served as matron for the institution. I folded up the one picture I had saved of the baby's father and stuffed it into the little wooden box they had given me at the hospital to hold the umbilical cord.

As soon as I'd managed to get the baby into a day care center, I went straight to the Akebono Housekeeping Agency and arranged for an interview. It was the only job I could think of that matched my limited skills.

Shortly before Root entered elementary school, my mother and I reconciled: a fancy backpack arrived in the mail for him. This happened at the same time that I had left the single mothers' home and set up house for ourselves. My mother was still managing the wedding hall. But just as our troubles seemed to be over and I'd begun to see how comforting it could be to have a grandmother for my child, my mother suddenly died of a brain hemorrhage—which may be why I was even happier than Root himself when I saw the Professor hug him.

The three of us soon fell into a pleasant routine. There was no change in my schedule or workload, other than making more food for dinner. Fridays were the busiest, as I had to prepare food for the weekend and store it away in the freezer. I would make meat loaf and mashed potatoes, or poached fish and vegetables, and explain repeatedly what went with what and how to defrost the food, although the Professor never quite figured out how to use the microwave. Nevertheless, when I arrived on Monday morning, all the food I'd prepared was gone. The meat loaf and fish had somehow been thawed and eaten, and the dirty dishes had been washed and put away in the cupboard. I was sure that the old woman took care of the Professor when I wasn't there, but as long as I was around, she never made an appearance. I had no idea why she had placed such a firm restriction on communication between her house and the Professor's, but I decided that my next challenge was to figure out how to get to know her.

The Professor's problems, on the other hand, were all mathematical. He never seemed particularly proud of his accomplishments, even when he had spent a long time solving an equation that had won both the prize money and my praise.

"It was just a little puzzle," he would say, "a game"; and his tone sounded more sad than modest. "The person who made the problem already knew the answer. Solving a problem for which you know there's an answer is like climbing a mountain with a guide, along a trail someone else has laid. In mathematics, the truth is somewhere out there in a place no one knows, beyond all the beaten paths. And it's not always at the top of the mountain. It might be in a crack on the smoothest cliff or somewhere deep in the valley."

In the afternoon, when he heard Root's voice at the door, the Professor came out of his study, no matter how absorbed he was in his work. Though he had always hated to have his "thinking" interrupted, he now seemed more than willing to give it up for my son.

Most days, however, Root simply delivered his backpack and went off to the park to play baseball with his friends, and the Professor would retreat dejectedly to his study.

So the Professor seemed particularly cheerful when the weather turned rainy and he was able to help Root with his math homework.

"I think I'm a little smarter when I'm in the Professor's office," Root told me. There were no bookshelves in the little apartment where we lived, so the Professor's study, with its stacks of volumes lining the walls, seemed magical to him. The Professor would sweep aside the notebooks and clips and eraser shavings on his desk to make space for Root, and then he would open the textbook.

How is it possible for a professor of advanced mathematics to teach a child in elementary school? The Professor was especially gifted, he had the most wonderful way of teaching fractions and ratios and volume, and it occurred to me that all parents should be giving this kind of help to their children.

Whether it was a word problem or just a simple calculation, the Professor made Root read it aloud first.

"$353 \times 840 = \ldots$

"$6239 \div 23 = \ldots$

"$4.62 + 2.74 = \ldots$

"$5\frac{2}{7} - 2\frac{1}{7} = \ldots$"

"A problem has a rhythm of its own, just like a piece of music," the Professor said. "Once you get the rhythm, you get the sense of the problem as a whole, and you can see where the traps might be waiting."

And so Root read in a loud, clear voice: "I bought two handkerchiefs and two pairs of socks for ¥380. Two handkerchiefs and five pairs of socks cost ¥710. How much did each handkerchief and each pair of socks cost?"

"So, where do we start?" asked the Professor.

"Well, it seems pretty hard."

"You're right. This is the trickiest one in your homework today, but you read it well. The problem consists of three sentences. The handkerchiefs and socks appear three times each, and you had the rhythm just right: so many handkerchiefs . . . so many socks . . . so many yen; handkerchiefs . . . socks . . . yen. You made a boring problem sound just like a poem."

The Professor was unstinting with his praise for Root. He never seemed to lose patience when time passed and they were making little progress; and like a miner sifting a speck of gold from the muddy river bottom, he always found some small virtue to compliment, even when Root was stuck.

"Well then, suppose we draw a picture of this little shopping trip. First, there are two handkerchiefs; then two pairs of socks—"

"Those aren't socks!" Root interrupted. "They look more like overweight caterpillars. Let me draw them."

"I see what you mean. That does look more like a caterpillar."

"He bought the same number of handkerchiefs the second time but more socks. Five pairs is a lot to draw. . . . Mine are starting to look like caterpillars, too."

"No, they're fine. And you're right, only the number of socks increases, along with the price. Why don't we check to see how much the price went up?"

"So, you'd subtract ¥380 from ¥710. . . ."

"Always show your work, and do it neatly."

"I usually just scribble on the back of scrap paper."

"But every formula and every number has meaning, and you should treat them accordingly, don't you think?"

I was sitting on the bed, doing some mending. Whenever they started Root's homework, I tried to find something to do in the study in order to be near them. I would iron the Professor's shirts, or work on a stain in the rug, or snip string beans for supper. If I was working in the kitchen and heard their laughter drift in from the other room, I felt terribly excluded—and I suppose I wanted to be there when anyone was showing kindness to my son.

The sound of the rain seemed louder in the study, as if the sky were actually lower there. The room was completely private, thanks to the lush greenery that grew up around the house, and there was no need to close the curtains even after dark. Their reflections appeared dimly in windowpanes, and on rainy days the musty smell in the study was stronger than usual.

"That's right! Then it's just a matter of simple division and you've got it."

"So, you get the price of the socks first: ¥110."

"Okay, but you've got to be careful now. The handkerchiefs seem innocent, but they may turn out to be tricky."

"Right. But it's easier to do the sums when the numbers are small."

The desk was a bit too high, and Root was forced to sit up very straight as he leaned over his problem, a well-chewed pencil clutched tightly in his hand. The Professor sat back, legs crossed and looking relaxed, and his hand drifted to his unshaven chin from time to time as he watched Root work. He was no longer a frail old man, nor a scholar lost in his thoughts, but the rightful protector of a child. Their profiles seemed to come together, superimposed on one another, forming a single line. The gentle patter of the rain was punctuated by the scratching of pencil on paper.

"Can I write out the equations separately like this? Our teacher gets mad if we don't combine them all into one big formula."

"If you're doing them carefully and correctly, he has no reason to get mad."

"Okay, let's see. . . . 110 times 2 is 220. Subtract that from 380. . . . That's 160 . . . 160 divided by 2 . . . is 80. That's it. One handkerchief costs ¥80."

"That's right! Well done!"

As the Professor rubbed Root's head, Root glanced up into his face, not wanting to miss the look of approval and pleasure.

"I'd like to give you a problem myself," said the Professor. "Would you mind?"

"What?"

"No long faces now. Since we're studying together, I feel like playing the teacher and giving you homework."

"That's not fair," said Root.

"It's just one little problem. All right? Here it is: What is the sum of all the numbers from 1 to 10?"

"Okay, I'll let you give me homework if you'll do something for me. I want you to get the radio fixed."

"The radio?"

"That's right. I want to listen to the ball games. You don't have a TV and the radio's broken. And we're coming down to the pennant race."

"Oh, I see . . . baseball." The Professor let out a long, slow breath, his hand still resting on Root's head. "What team do you like?" he asked at last.

"Can't you tell from my hat?" Root said, picking up the cap

he'd left with his backpack and pulling it over his head. "The Tigers!"

"The Tigers? Is that right? The Tigers," the Professor murmured. "Enatsu! Yutaka Enatsu, best pitcher of all time."

"Yes! Good thing you don't like the Giants. Okay, we've got to get the radio fixed," Root insisted. The Professor seemed to be muttering something to himself, but I closed the lid of the sewing box and stood up to announce it was time for dinner.

3

I finally managed to get the Professor out of the house. Since I'd come to work, he had not so much as set foot in the garden, let alone gone for a real outing, and I thought some fresh air would be good for him.

"It's beautiful outside today," I said, coaxing him. "It makes you want to go out, get some sun." The Professor was ensconced in his easy chair with a book. "Why don't we take a walk in the park and then stop in at the barbershop?"

"And why would we do that?" he said, glancing up at me over his reading glasses.

"No particular reason. The cherry blossoms are just over in the park and the dogwood is about to bloom. And a haircut might feel good."

"I feel fine like this."

"A walk would get your circulation going, and that might help you come up with some good ideas for your formulas."

"There's no connection between the arteries in the legs and the ones in the head."

"Well, you'd be much handsomer if you took care of your hair."

"Waste of time," he said, but eventually my persistence got the better of him and he closed his book. The only shoes in the cupboard by the door were old leather ones covered in a thin layer of mold. "You'll stay with me?" he asked several times as I was cleaning them off. "You can't just leave me while I'm having my hair cut and come home."

"Don't worry. I'll stay with you the whole time." No matter how much I polished, the shoes were still dull.

I wasn't sure what to do with the notes the Professor had clipped all over his body. If we left them on, people were bound to stare, but since he didn't seem to care, I decided to leave them alone.

The Professor marched along, staring down at his feet, without a glance at the blue sky overhead or the sights we passed along the way. The walk did not seem to relax him, he was more tense than usual.

"Look," I'd say, "the cherry blossoms are in full bloom." But he only muttered to himself. Out in the open air, he seemed somehow older.

We decided to go to the barbershop first. The barber recoiled at the sight of the Professor's strange suit, but he turned out to be a kind man. He realized quickly that there must be a reason for the notes, and after that he treated the Professor like any other customer. "You're lucky to have your daughter with you," he said, assuming we were related. Neither of us corrected him. I sat on the sofa with the men waiting in line for their haircuts.

Perhaps the Professor had an unpleasant memory of going to the barber. Whatever the reason, he was clearly nervous from the moment the cape was fastened around his neck. His face went stiff, his fingers dug into the arms of the chair, and deep creases lined his forehead. The barber brought up several harmless topics in an attempt to put him at ease, but it was no use.

"What's your shoe size?" the Professor blurted out. "What's your telephone number?" The room fell silent.

Though he could see me in the mirror, he craned around from time to time, checking to see that I'd kept my promise to stay with him. When the Professor moved his head, the barber was forced to stop cutting, but he would wait patiently and then go back to work. I smiled and gave a little wave to reassure the Professor that I was still there.

The white clippings of hair fell in clumps on the cape and then scattered to the floor. As he cut and combed away, did the barber suspect that the brain inside this snowy head could list all the prime numbers up to a hundred million? And did the customers on the sofa, waiting impatiently for the strange old man to depart, have any notion of the special bond between my birthday and the Professor's wristwatch? For some reason, I felt a secret pride in knowing these things, and I smiled at the Professor just a bit more brightly in the mirror.

After the barbershop, we sat on a bench in the park and drank a can of coffee. There was a sandbox nearby, and a fountain and some tennis courts. When the wind blew, the petals from the cherry trees floated around us and the dappled sunlight danced on the Professor's face. The notes on his jacket fluttered restlessly, and he stared down into the can as if he'd been given some mysterious potion.

"I was right—you look handsome, and more manly."

"That's quite enough of that," said the Professor. For once he smelled of shaving cream rather than of paper.

"What kind of mathematics did you study at the university?" I asked. I had little confidence that I would understand his answer; maybe I brought up the subject of numbers as a way of thanking him for coming out with me.

"It's sometimes called the 'Queen of Mathematics,'" he said, after taking a sip of his coffee. "Noble and beautiful, like a queen, but cruel as a demon. In other words, I studied the whole numbers we all know, 1, 2, 3, 4, 5, 6, 7 . . . and the relationships between them."

His choice of the word *queen* surprised me—as if he were telling a fairy tale. We could hear the sound of a tennis ball bouncing in the distance. The joggers and bikers and mothers pushing strollers glanced at the Professor as they passed but then quickly looked away.

"You look for the relationships between them?"

"Yes, that's right. I uncovered propositions that existed out there long before we were born. It's like copying truths from God's notebook, though we aren't always sure where to find this notebook or when it will be open." As he said the words "out there," he gestured toward the distant point at which he stared when he was doing his "thinking."

"For example, when I was studying at Cambridge I worked on

Artin's conjecture about cubic forms with whole-number coefficients. I used the 'circle method' and employed algebraic geometry, whole number theory, and the Diophantine equation. I was looking for a cubic form that didn't conform to the Artin conjecture. . . . In the end, I found a proof that worked for a certain type of form under a specific set of conditions."

The Professor picked up a branch and began to scratch something in the dirt. There were numbers, and letters, and some mysterious symbols, all arranged in neat lines. I couldn't understand a word he had said, but there seemed to be great clarity in his reasoning, as if he were pushing through to a profound truth. The nervous old man I'd watched at the barbershop had disappeared, and his manner now was dignified. The withered stick gracefully carved the Professor's thoughts into the dry earth, and before long the lacy pattern of the formula was spread out at our feet.

"May I tell you about something I discovered?" I could hardly believe the words had come out of my mouth, but the Professor's hand fell still. Overcome by the beauty of his delicate patterns, perhaps I'd wanted to take part; and I was absolutely sure he would show great respect, even for the humblest discovery.

"The sum of the divisors of 28 is 28."

"Indeed . . . ," he said. And there, next to his outline of the Artin conjecture, he wrote: $28 = 1 + 2 + 4 + 7 + 14$. "A perfect number."

"Perfect number?" I murmured, savoring the sound of the words.

"The smallest perfect number is 6: $6 = 1 + 2 + 3$."

"Oh! Then they're not so special after all."

"On the contrary, a number with this kind of perfection is rare indeed. After 28, the next one is 496: $496 = 1 + 2 + 4 + 8 + 16 + 31$

+ 62 + 124 + 248. After that, you have 8,128; and the next one after that is 33,550,336. Then 8,589,869,056. The farther you go, the more difficult they are to find"—though he had easily followed the trail into the billions!

"Naturally, the sums of the divisors of numbers *other* than perfect numbers are either greater or less than the numbers themselves. When the sum is greater, it's called an 'abundant number,' and when it's less, it's a 'deficient number.' Marvelous names, don't you think? The divisors of 18— + 2 + 3 + 6 + 9—equal 21, so it's an abundant number. But 14 is deficient: 1 + 2 + 7 = 10."

I tried picturing 18 and 14, but now that I'd heard the Professor's explanation, they were no longer simply numbers. Eighteen secretly carried a heavy burden, while 14 fell mute in the face of its terrible lack.

"There are lots of deficient numbers that are just one larger than the sum of their divisors, but there are no abundant numbers that are just one smaller than the sum of theirs. Or rather, no one has ever found one."

"Why is that?"

"The answer is written in God's notebook," said the Professor.

Everything around us was glowing in the sunlight; even the dried shells of the insects floating in the fountain seemed to glitter. The most important of the Professor's notes—the one that read "My memory lasts only eighty minutes"—had come loose, and I reached over to adjust the clip.

"I'll show you one more thing about perfect numbers," he said, swinging the branch and drawing his legs under the bench to make more room on the ground. "You can express them as the sum of *consecutive* natural numbers."

$$6 = 1 + 2 + 3$$

$$28 = 1 + 2 + 3 + 4 + 5 + 6 + 7$$

$$496 = 1 + 2 + 3 + 4 + 5 + 6 + 7 + 8 + 9 + 10 + 11 + 12 + 13 + 14$$
$$+ 15 + 16 + 17 + 18 + 19 + 20 + 21 + 22 + 23 + 24 + 25 + 26$$
$$+ 27 + 28 + 29 + 30 + 31$$

The Professor reached out to complete the long equation. The numbers unfolded in a simple, straight line, polished and clean. The subtle formula for the Artin conjecture and the plain line of factors for the number 28 blended seamlessly, surrounding us where we sat on the bench. The figures became stitches in the elaborate pattern woven in the dirt. I sat utterly still, afraid I might accidentally erase part of the design. It seemed as though the secret of the universe had miraculously appeared right here at our feet, as though God's notebook had opened under our bench.

"Well then," the Professor said at last. "We should probably be getting home."

"Yes, we should," I said, nodding. "Root will be there soon."

"Root?"

"My son. He's ten years old. The top of his head is flat, so we call him Root."

"Is that so? You have a son? We can't dawdle then. You should be there when he gets home from school." With that, he stood to go.

Just then, there was a cry from the sandbox. A little girl stood sobbing, a toy shovel clutched in her hand. Instantly, the Professor was at her side, bending over to comfort her. He tenderly brushed the sand from her dress.

Suddenly, the child's mother appeared and pushed the Professor away, picking the girl up and practically running off with her. The Professor was left standing in the sandbox. I watched him from behind, unsure how to help. The cherry blossoms fluttered down, mingling with the numbers in the dirt.

"I did the problem and I got it right. So now you have to keep your promise and fix the radio." These were the first words out of Root's mouth as he came through the door. "Here, look," he said, holding out his math notebook.

$$1 + 2 + 3 + 4 + 5 + 6 + 7 + 8 + 9 + 10 = 55$$

The Professor studied Root's work as though it were a sophisticated proof. Unable to recall why he had assigned this problem or what connection it had to repairing the radio, he was perhaps looking for an answer in the sum itself.

The Professor carefully avoided asking us questions about things that had happened more than eighty minutes ago. We would have happily explained the meaning of the homework and the radio if he had asked, but he preferred to examine the facts before him and draw his own conclusions. Because he had been—and in many ways still was—such a brilliant man, he no doubt understood the nature of his memory problem. It wasn't pride that prevented him from asking for help but a deep aversion to causing more trouble than necessary for those of us who lived in the normal world. When I realized why he was so reluctant to bring up the subject of his memory, I decided I would say as little as possible about it, too.

"You've added up the numbers from 1 to 10," he said at last.

"I got it right, didn't I? I checked it over and over, I'm sure it's right."

"Indeed it is!"

"Good! Then let's go get the radio fixed."

"Now just a minute," said the Professor, coughing quietly as if to give himself time to think. "I wonder if you could explain to me how you got the answer?"

"That's easy! You just add them up."

"That's a straightforward way to do it; perfectly reliable, and no one can argue with that." Root nodded proudly. "But think for a minute: what would you do if a teacher, say, a *mean* teacher, asked you to add the numbers from 1 to 100?"

"I'd add them up, of course."

"Naturally you would. You're a good boy, and a hard worker. So I'm sure you'd come up with the right answer for 1 to 100, too. But what if that teacher was really cruel and made you find the sum for 1 to 1,000? Or 1 to 10,000? You'd be adding, adding, and adding forever while that teacher laughed at you. What would you do then?" Root shook his head. "But you can't let that evil teacher get to you," the Professor continued. "You've got to show him you're the better man."

"But how do you do that?"

"You need to find a simpler way to get the answer that works no matter how big the numbers get. If you can find it, then I'll get the radio fixed."

"That's not fair!" Root objected, kicking his chair leg. "That wasn't part of the deal."

"Root!" I interrupted. "Is that any way to act?" But the Professor didn't seem to notice his outburst.

"A problem isn't finished just because you've found the right answer. There's another way to get to 55; wouldn't you like to find it?"

"Not really . . . ," said Root, sulking.

"All right, here's what we'll do. The radio is old, and it may take them a while to get it working again. So how about a contest to see whether you can find another way to get the sum before the radio is fixed?"

"Okay," said Root. "But I don't see how I'm going to do it. What other way *is* there besides just adding them up?"

"Who'd have guessed you're such a quitter," the Professor scolded. "Giving up before you've even tried."

"Fine. I'll try. But I can't promise I'll figure it out before the radio's done. I've got a lot of other stuff to do."

"We'll see," said the Professor, and he rubbed Root's head as he always did. "Oh!" he said suddenly. "I've got to make a note." He took a sheet of paper, wrote out their agreement, then clipped it to his lapel. There was something smooth and controlled in the way he held the pen and wrote the note, so different from his usual clumsy manner.

"But you have to promise to finish your homework before the game comes on; and to turn it off during dinner; and not to disturb the Professor while he's working." Root nodded grumpily as I listed each condition.

"I know," he said, "but it'll be worth it. The Tigers are good this year, not like last year and the year before when they were in last place. They even won their first game against the Giants."

"Is that right? Hanshin's having a good year?" the Professor said. "What's Enatsu's ERA?" The Professor looked back and forth between us. "How many strikeouts does he have?" Root waited for a moment before answering.

"They traded Enatsu," he said at last. "That was before I was born, and he's retired now." A jolt shot through the Professor and then he was still.

I had never seen him so distressed. He had always calmly accepted the way his memory failed him, but this time was different. This time he couldn't ignore the facts. Seeing him this way, I even forgot to worry about Root, who had received a shock of his own at causing the Professor such pain.

"But even after they traded him to the Carp, he was the best in the league." I hoped this would reassure him, but this new information distressed him even more.

"The Carp? What do you mean? How could Enatsu wear anything but the Hanshin pinstripes?"

He sat down and rested his elbows on the desk, running his hands through his freshly cut hair. Tiny clippings fell on his notebook. This time it was Root who rubbed the Professor's head. He smoothed the mussed hair as if trying to undo the trouble he'd caused.

Root and I were quiet on the way home that evening. When I asked him whether the Tigers had a game, his answer was barely audible.

"Who are they playing?"

"Taiyo."

"You think they'll win?"

"Who knows."

The lights were out in the barbershop and the park was empty. The formulas the Professor had scratched in the dirt were hidden in the shadows.

"I shouldn't have said those things," Root said. "But I didn't know he liked Enatsu so much."

"I didn't know, either," I said. And then, though it was probably wrong of me, I added, "Don't worry, it will all be back to normal by tomorrow morning. In the Professor's mind, Enatsu will be the Tigers' ace again and he won't remember anything about the Carp."

The problem that the Professor had posed to Root proved to be almost as difficult as the one that Enatsu had presented for all of us.

As the Professor had predicted, the man at the repair shop said that he had never seen such an old radio and that he wasn't sure he could fix it. But if he could, he said, he would try to have it done in a week's time. So every day, when I got home from work, I spent my evening looking for another way to find the sum of the natural numbers from 1 to 10. Root should have been working on the problem, too, but perhaps because he was upset over the incident with Enatsu, he gave up almost immediately and left me to find a solution. For my part, I was anxious to please the Professor, and I certainly didn't want to disappoint him any more than we already had. But the only way to please him, I suspected, was through numbers.

I began by reading the problem aloud, just as the Professor had insisted Root do with his homework: "$1 + 2 + 3 + \ldots 9 + 10$ is 55. $1 + 2 + 3 + \ldots$" But this didn't seem to be much help—except to show that a simple equation could conceal a terribly difficult problem.

Next I tried writing out the numbers from 1 to 10 both horizontally and vertically and grouping them by odds and evens, primes and non-primes, and so on. I worked on the problem with matches and marbles, and when I was at the Professor's house, I jotted down numbers on the back of any piece of scrap paper, always looking for a clue.

To find an amicable number, all you had to do was perform the same sort of calculation again and again. If you had enough time, you'd eventually succeed. But this was different. I was constantly starting off in a new direction, looking for another way to approach the problem, only to wind up at a dead end, confused. To be honest, I wasn't always even sure of what I was trying to do. At times I seemed to be going around in circles and at others almost backward, away from a solution; and in the end, I was often simply staring at the scrap paper.

I'm not sure why I became so absorbed in a child's math problem with no practical value. At first, I was conscious of wanting to please the Professor, but gradually that feeling faded and I realized it had become a battle between the problem and me. When I woke in the morning, the equation was waiting—$1+2+3+\ldots 9+10 = 55$—and it followed me all through the day, as though it had burned itself into my retina and could not be ignored.

At first, it was just a small distraction, but it quickly became an obsession. Only a few people know the mystery concealed in this formula, and the rest of us go to our graves without even suspecting there is a secret to be revealed. But by some whim of fate, I had found it, and now knocked at the door, asking to be let in. Though I had never suspected it, from the moment I'd been dispatched by the Akebono Housekeeping Agency, I had been on a mission toward that door . . .

"Do I look like the Professor?" I asked Root, my hand pressed to my temple and a pencil clenched in my fingers. That day, I had covered the back of every flyer and handbill in the house, but I'd made no progress.

"No, not a bit," Root said. "When the Professor's solving a problem, he doesn't talk to himself the way you do, and he doesn't pull out his hair. His body's there but his mind goes somewhere else. And besides," he added, "his problems are a *lot* harder!"

"I know! But whose problem is this anyway? Maybe you could stop reading your baseball books for a minute and help me."

"But you're three times as old as I am! And besides, it's a crazy problem anyway."

"Showing the factors was progress. That was thanks to the Professor, wasn't it?"

"I guess so," said Root, looking at my work on the backs of the advertisements and nodding as though he found everything in proper order.

"I think you're on the right track," he said at last.

"Some help you are!" I laughed.

"Better than nothing," he said, turning back to his book.

Since he was very small, he'd often had to console me when I came home from work in tears—when I'd been accused of stealing, or called incompetent, or had the food I'd made thrown away right in front of me. "You're beautiful, Momma," he'd say, his voice full of conviction, "It'll be okay." This was what he always said when he comforted me. "I'm a beauty?" I would ask, and he'd say, feigning astonishment, "Sure you are. Didn't you know?" More than once I'd pretended to be crying just to hear these words; and he'd always play along willingly.

"But you know what I think?" he said suddenly. "When you're adding up the numbers, 10 is odd man out."

"Why do you say that?"

"Well, 10's the only one with two places."

He was right, of course. I had analyzed the numbers in many ways, but had not thought about how each number was special, different. When I looked at them again, it seemed terribly strange that I'd never noticed how odd 10 looked lined up against the others—the only one among them that could not be written without picking up the pencil.

"If you got rid of ten, you'd have a number in the center spot, which might be good."

"What do you mean, 'center spot'?"

"You'd know if you came to the last Parents' Day. We were doing gymnastics—that's my best sport—and in the middle of the exercise the teacher said, 'Double lines, face center.' The guy in the middle held up his arms and the rest of us lined up facing him. There were nine of us, so the guy in fifth place was the center, and the lines were even. For 10 it doesn't work. If you add just one guy, you don't have a center."

So now I tried leaving 10 aside and lining up the rest of the numbers. I circled five in the center, with four numbers before it and four after. The 5 stood, arms proudly extended, enjoying the attention of all the others.

And at that moment I experienced a kind of revelation for the first time in my life, a sort of miracle. In the midst of a vast field of numbers, a straight path opened before my eyes. A light was shining at the end, leading me on, and I knew then that it was the path to enlightenment.

· · · ·

The radio came back from the repair shop on Friday, the twenty-fourth of April, the day the Tigers were scheduled to play the Dragons. We put it on the center of the table and sat around it. Root twisted the knobs, and the broadcast of the game crackled out from the static. The signal was weak, but there was no doubt it was the baseball game—and the first sign of life from the outside world that had made its way into the house since my arrival. We let out a little cheer.

"I had no idea you could get baseball on this radio," said the Professor.

"Of course! You can get it on any radio."

"My brother bought it for me a long time ago, for practicing English conversation. I thought it would only pick up English."

"So you've never listened to the Tigers?" Root said.

"No, and I haven't got a TV, either . . . ," murmured the Professor, as if confessing something awful. "I've never seen a baseball game."

"I don't believe it!" Root blurted out, nearly shouting.

"I know the rules, though," the Professor said, a bit defensively. But Root was not to be appeased.

"How can you call yourself a Tigers fan?"

"But I am—a big fan. When I was in college, I went to the library at lunch to read the sports pages. But I did more than just read about baseball. You see, no other sport is captured so perfectly by its statistics, its numbers. I analyzed the data for the Hanshin players, their batting averages and ERAs, and by tracking the changes, even miniscule shifts, I could picture the flow of the games in my head."

"And that was fun?"

"Of course it was. Even without the radio, I could keep every detail fixed in my mind: Enatsu's first victory as a pro in 1967—he beat the Carp with ten strikeouts; the game in 1973 when he pitched an extra-innings no-hitter and then hit a walk-off home run himself." Just at that moment, the announcer on the radio mentioned the name of the Tigers starting pitcher, Kasai. "So when is Enatsu scheduled to pitch?" the Professor asked.

"He's a little farther on in the rotation," Root answered without missing a beat. It surprised me to see him acting so grown-up. We'd promised that where Enatsu was concerned, we'd do anything to keep up the illusion. Still, it made us uncomfortable to lie to the Professor, and it was hard to know whether it was really in his best interest. But we could not bear to upset him again.

"We can tell him that Enatsu's back in the dugout, or that he's throwing in the bullpen," Root had said.

Since Enatsu had retired long before Root was born, he'd gone to the library to find out about him. He learned that he had a career record of 206 wins, 158 losses, and 193 saves, with 2,987 strikeouts. He'd hit a home run in his second at bat as a pro; he had short fingers for a pitcher. He'd struck out his great rival, Sadaharu Oh, more than any other pitcher, but he'd also surrendered the most home runs to him. In the course of their rivalry, however, he'd never hit Oh with a pitch. During the 1968 season, he set a world record with 401 strikeouts, and after the 1975 season (the year the Professor's memory came to an end), he'd been traded to the Nankai Hawks.

Root had wanted to know more about Enatsu, so he would seem more real to *both* of them as they listened to the cheers on the radio. While I had been struggling with the "homework" problem, he had been seeing to the Enatsu problem. Then one day, as I was flipping through a copy of *Baseball Players Illustrated* that he'd brought home from the library, I was stunned to find a picture of Enatsu, and see on his uniform the number 28. When he'd graduated from Osaka Gakuin and joined the Tigers, he'd been offered the three available numbers: 1, 13, and 28. He'd chosen 28. Enatsu had played his whole career with a perfect number on his back!

That evening, after dinner, we presented our solution. We stood before the Professor, pen and paper in hand, and bowed.

"This is the problem you gave us," said Root. "Find the sum of the numbers from 1 to 10 without adding them." He cleared his throat and then, just as we'd arranged the night before, I held the notebook while he wrote the numbers 1 to 9 in a line, adding 10 farther down on the page. "We already know the answer. It's 55. I added them up and that's what I got. But you didn't care about the answer."

The Professor folded his arms and listened intently, as if hanging on to Root's every word.

"So we decided to think about 1 to 9 first, and forget about 10 for right now. The number 5 is in the middle, so it's the . . . uh . . ."

"Average," I whispered in his ear.

"Right, the average. We haven't learned averages yet, so Momma helped me with that part. If you add up 1 through 9 and divide by 9 you get 5 . . . so $5 \times 9 = 45$, that's the sum of the numbers 1 to 9. And now it's time to bring back the 10."

$5 \times 9 + 10 = 55$

Root took the pen and wrote the equation on the pad.

The Professor sat studying what he had written, and I was sure then that my moment of inspiration must look laughably crude to him. I'd known from the start that I would never be able to extract something sublime and true from my poor brain cells, no chance of imagining something that would please a real mathematician.

But then the Professor stood up and began to applaud as warmly and enthusiastically as if we had just solved Fermat's theorem. He clapped for a long time, filling the little house with his approval.

"Wonderful! It's magnificent, Root." He folded Root in his arms, half crushing him.

"Okay, okay. I can't breathe," Root mumbled, his words nearly lost in the Professor's embrace.

He was determined to make this skinny boy with the flat head understand how beautiful his discovery was, but as I stood watching Root's triumph, I secretly felt proud of my own contribution. I looked at the line of figures Root had written. $5 \times 9 + 10 = 55$. And even though I'd never really studied mathematics, I knew that the formula became more impressive if you restated it in abstract form:

$$\frac{n(n-1)}{2} + n$$

It was a splendid discovery, and the clarity and purity of the solution was even more extraordinary in light of the confusion it had emerged from, as if I'd unearthed a shard of crystal from the floor of a dark cave. I laughed quietly, realizing that I'd praised myself adequately, even if the Professor's compliments had been directed elsewhere.

Root was finally released, and we bowed again like two schol-ars who had just finished their presentation at an academic con-ference.

That day, the Tigers lost 2–3 to the Dragons. They had taken a two-run lead on a triple by Wada, but the Dragons responded with back-to-back home runs and won the game.

4

The Professor loved prime numbers more than anything in the world. I'd been vaguely aware of their existence, but it never occurred to me that they could be the object of someone's deepest affection. He was tender and attentive and respectful; by turns he would caress them or prostrate himself before them; he never strayed far from his prime numbers. Whether at his desk or at the dinner table, when he talked about numbers, primes were most likely to make an appearance. At first, it was hard to see their appeal. They seemed so stubborn, resisting division by any number but one and themselves. Still, as we were swept up in the Professor's enthusiasm, we gradually came to understand his devotion, and the primes began to seem more real, as though we could reach out and touch them. I'm sure they meant something different to each of us, but as soon as the Professor would mention prime numbers, we would look at each other with conspiratorial smiles. Just as the thought of a caramel can cause your mouth to water, the mere mention of prime numbers made us anxious to know more about their secrets.

Evening was a precious time for the three of us. The vague tension around my morning arrival—which for the Professor was always our first encounter—had dissipated, and Root livened up our quiet days. I suppose that's why I'll always remember the Professor's face in the evening, in profile, lit by the setting sun.

Inevitably, the Professor repeated himself when he talked about prime numbers. But Root and I had promised each other that we would never tell him, even if we had heard the same thing several times before—a promise we took as seriously as our agreement to hide the truth about Enatsu. No matter how weary we were of hearing a story, we always made an effort to listen attentively. We felt we owed that to the Professor, who had put so much effort into treating the two of us as real mathematicians. But our main concern was to avoid confusing him. Any kind of uncertainty caused him pain, so we were determined to hide the time that had passed and the memories he'd lost. Biting our tongues was the least we could do.

But the truth was, we were almost never bored when he spoke of mathematics. Though he often returned to the topic of prime numbers—the proof that there were an infinite number of them, or a code that had been devised based on primes, or the most enormous known examples, or twin primes, or the Mersenne primes—the slightest change in the shape of his argument could make you see something you had never understood before. Even a difference in the weather or in his tone of voice seemed to cast these numbers in a different light.

To me, the appeal of prime numbers had something to do with the fact that you could never predict when one would appear. They seemed to be scattered along the number line at any place that took their fancy. The farther you get from zero, the harder they are to find, and no theory or rule could predict where they will turn up next. It was this tantalizing puzzle that held the Professor captive.

"Let's try finding the prime numbers up to 100," the Professor said one day when Root had finished his homework. He took his pencil and began making a list: 2, 3, 5, 7, 11, 13, 17, 19, 23, 29, 31, 37, 41, 43, 47, 53, 59, 61, 67, 71, 73, 79, 83, 89, 97.

It always amazed me how easily numbers seemed to flow from the Professor, at any time, under any circumstances. How could these trembling hands, which could barely turn on the microwave, make such precise numbers of all shapes and sizes?

I also liked the way he wrote his numbers with his little stub of a pencil. The 4 was so round it looked like a knot of ribbon, and the 5 was leaning so far forward it seemed about to tip over. They weren't lined up very neatly, but they all had a certain personality. The Professor's lifelong affection for numbers could be seen in every figure he wrote.

"So, what do you see?" He tended to begin with this sort of general question.

"They're scattered all over the place." Root usually answered first. "And 2 is the only one that's even." For some reason, he always noticed the odd man out.

"You're right. Two is the only even prime. It's the leadoff batter for the infinite team of prime numbers after it."

"That must be awfully lonely," said Root.

"Don't worry," said the Professor. "If it gets lonely, it has lots of company with the other even numbers."

"But some of them come in pairs, like 17 and 19, and 41 and 43," I said, not wanting to be shown up by Root.

"A very astute observation," said the Professor. "Those are known as 'twin primes.'"

I wondered why ordinary words seemed so exotic when they were used in relation to numbers. *Amicable numbers* or *twin primes* had a precise quality about them, and yet they sounded as though they'd been taken straight out of a poem. In my mind, the twins had matching outfits and stood holding hands as they waited in the number line.

"As the numbers get bigger, the distance between primes increases as well, and it becomes more difficult to find twins. So we don't know yet whether twin primes are infinite the way prime numbers themselves are." As he spoke, the Professor circled the consecutive pairs.

Among the many things that made the Professor an excellent teacher was the fact that he wasn't afraid to say "we don't know." For the Professor, there was no shame in admitting you didn't have the answer, it was a necessary step toward the truth. It was as important to teach us about the unknown or the unknowable as it was to teach us what had already been safely proven.

"If numbers never end, then there should always be more twins, right?"

"That makes sense, Root. But when you get to much bigger

numbers—a million or ten million—you're venturing into a waste-land where the primes are terribly far apart."

"A wasteland?"

"That's right, a desert. No matter how far you go, you don't find any. Just sand as far as the eye can see. The sun shines down mercilessly, your throat is parched, your eyes glaze over. Then you think you see one, a prime number at last, and you go running toward it—only to find that it's just a mirage, nothing but hot wind. Still, you refuse to give up, staggering on step by step, determined to continue the search . . . until you see it at last, the oasis of another prime number, a place of rest and cool, clear water. . . ."

The rays of the setting sun stretched far into the room. Root traced the circles around the twin primes as the steam from the rice cooker floated in from the kitchen. The Professor stared through the window as if he were looking out at the desert, though all he could really see was his tiny, neglected garden.

The thing the Professor hated most in the whole world was a crowd, which is why he was so reluctant to leave the house. Sta-tions, trains, department stores, movie theaters, shopping malls—any place people gathered in large numbers was unbearable for him. There was something fundamentally incompatible between crushing, random crowds and pure mathematical beauty.

The Professor wanted peace, though that didn't necessarily mean complete silence. Apparently, he was not disturbed by Root when he ran down the hall or turned up the volume on the radio. What he needed was internal calm uninterrupted by the outside world.

When he had solved a contest problem from one of his journals and was making a clean copy to put in the mail, you could often hear him murmur, "How peaceful . . ." He seemed to be perfectly calm in these moments, as though everything were in its rightful place, with nothing left to add or subtract. "Peaceful" was, to him, the highest compliment.

When he was in a good mood, he would sit at the kitchen table and watch me making dinner; and if I were making dumplings, he would look on with something approaching wonder. I would take a dumpling skin in the palm of my hand, spoon on a bit of filling, and then pinch up the edges before setting it on the platter. A simple process, but he was completely absorbed by it, watching me until the last dumpling had been stuffed. I have to admit that the scene struck me as so funny that I hardly could keep from laughing.

When I was done at last and the dumplings were neatly arranged on the plate, he would fold his hands on the table and nod solemnly. "How peaceful . . ."

On the sixth of May, at the end of the spring holidays, Root cut himself with a kitchen knife. The Professor did not take it well.

After the four-day break, I arrived at the Professor's house only to discover that the sink had been leaking and a puddle had spread into the hall. By the time I'd called to have the water shut off and hired a plumber to come in, I was probably a bit out of sorts. To make matters worse, the Professor had seemed more remote than ever, and no matter how often I pointed out my picture among the tags on his coat, he seemed confused or oblivious. By evening he had still not come out of his shell. While my irritation might have contributed to Root's accident, the Professor was in no way to blame.

Shortly after Root arrived from school, I realized that I'd run out of cooking oil. I was uneasy leaving the Professor and Root alone, so I talked to Root before I left.

"Do you think it's okay?"

"Is what okay?" he replied, almost curtly. It is hard to say exactly what worried me, I had no premonition, I was simply anxious about leaving the Professor in charge.

"I've never left you alone with the Professor and I was just wondering if that's okay—"

"Don't worry!" Root said, running off to the study to have his homework checked.

I was gone no more than twenty minutes, but when I opened the door, I knew immediately that something was wrong. I discovered the Professor, sobbing and moaning, crouched on the kitchen floor, holding Root in his arms.

"Root . . . Root . . . his hand!"

He could barely speak, and the more he tried to explain what had happened, the more incoherent he became. His teeth chattered and sweat poured down his face. I pried Root loose from his arms.

Root wasn't crying. He may have been trying to keep the Professor calm, or he may have been afraid I would be angry with him, but whatever the reason, he had been lying quietly in the Professor's arms, waiting for me to return. Their clothes were smeared with blood and the cut on Root's hand was still bleeding, but I could see right away that the Professor's panic was out of all proportion to Root's injury. The bleeding had nearly stopped, and

Root didn't appear to be in any pain. After I'd washed out the wound at the kitchen sink, I brought him a towel and told him to hold it on the cut. In the meantime, the Professor sat motionless on the floor, his arms frozen as if he were still holding Root. It seemed almost more urgent to look after him than it was to treat Root.

"Don't worry," I said, patting him gently on the back.

"How could this have happened? Such a sweet, good boy . . ."

"It's just a little cut. Boys hurt themselves all the time."

"But it's all my fault. He didn't do anything wrong. He didn't want to bother me, so he didn't say anything . . . he just sat there bleeding. . . ."

"It's no one's fault," I said.

"No, it's my fault. I tried to stop the bleeding, but I couldn't. . . . And then he got so pale, and I was afraid he'd stop breathing. . . ." He hid his face in his hands, covering the sweat and tears.

"Don't worry," I said again. "He'll be fine." As I rubbed his back, I realized that it was surprisingly broad and sturdy.

Neither Root nor the Professor were making much sense, but I finally managed to piece together what had happened: Root had finished his homework and was trying to peel an apple for a snack when he had cut himself between his thumb and index finger. The Professor insisted that Root had asked him for help with the apple, while Root maintained that he'd done the whole thing by himself. In any event, Root had tried to take care of the cut but he couldn't stop the bleeding, and the Professor had found him just as he'd begun to panic.

Unfortunately, the clinics in the neighborhood had already

closed for the day. The only doctor answering the phone was a pediatrician at a clinic behind the train station, who said he could see him right away. I helped the Professor up and dried his face, and at that point an astonishing change came over him. He hoisted Root onto his back, and though I tried to remind him that the child hadn't hurt his legs, he ran off to the doctor's carrying Root piggyback. To be honest, the ride seemed so rough that I was worried the wound would open up again. It could hardly have been easy for the Professor to carry a sixty-pound child on his back, but he was stronger than I'd thought. He charged along in his moldy shoes, gasping a bit from time to time, but holding Root's legs firmly under his arms. Root pulled his Tigers cap down over his eyes and buried his face in the Professor's back, less from pain than from the embarrassment of being seen. When we got to the clinic, the Professor pounded on the locked door, as though he were carrying a dying child on his back.

It took only two stitches to close the cut, but the Professor and I had to wait in the darkened corridor until they had finished the examination. They wanted to be sure Root hadn't severed a tendon.

The clinic was old and depressing. The ceiling was discolored, and the grimy slippers stuck to your feet. Yellowed posters on the walls gave instructions for weaning and inoculations. The only light in the hall was the dim bulb outside the X-ray room.

They'd said the test was just a precaution, but Root had been in the examination room for some time.

"Have you ever heard of triangular numbers?" the Professor

said, pointing at the radiation sign on the door of the X-ray room. It was shaped like a triangle.

"No," I said. He sounded calm now, but I could tell that he was still a little shaken.

"They're truly elegant," he said, beginning to draw dots on the back of a questionnaire that he'd picked up in the lobby.

"What do you make of these?"

"Well, let's see. It looks like neatly stacked firewood, or maybe rows of beans."

"That's right, the point is they're 'neatly' arranged. One in the first row, two in the second, three in the third. . . . It's the simplest way to form a triangle." I glanced at the dots on the page. The Professor's hand was trembling slightly. The black marks seemed to float up in the half-light. "So then, if we total up the number of dots in each triangle, we get 1, 3, 6, 10, 15, and 21. And if we write these as equations:

1

$1 + 2 = 3$

$1 + 2 + 3 = 6$

$1 + 2 + 3 + 4 = 10$

$1 + 2 + 3 + 4 + 5 = 15$

$1 + 2 + 3 + 4 + 5 + 6 = 21$

"In other words, a triangular number is the sum of all the natural numbers between 1 and a certain number. Then, if you put two of these triangles together, things get even more interesting. Why don't we look at the fourth one, 10, so we don't have to draw too many dots?"

It wasn't particularly cold in the hall, but the trembling in his hand had grown worse and the dots had slightly smudged. His whole being seemed concentrated in the tip of his pencil. A few of the notes on his suit were smeared with blood and now illegible.

"Look at this. When you put two of the four-row triangles together, you get a rectangle that is 4 dots high and 5 dots wide; and the total number in the rectangle is 4×5 or 20 dots. Do you see that? And if you divide that in half, you get $20 \div 2 = 10$, or the sum of the natural numbers from 1 to 4. Or, if you look at each line of the rectangle, you get:

1	2	3	4
+	+	+	+
4	3	2	1
5	5	5	5

"And once you know that, you can use this relationship to figure out the tenth triangle—the sum of the numbers from 1 to 10—or the hundredth or any other. For 1 to 10 it would be:

$$\frac{10 \times 11}{2} = 55$$

"And for 1 to 100,

$$\frac{100 \times 101}{2} = 5050$$

"And 1 to 1000,

$$\frac{1000 \times 1001}{2} = 500500$$

"And 1 to 10,000. . . ."

The pencil rolled out of his hand and fell at his feet. The Professor was crying. I believe it was the first time I saw him in tears, but I had the feeling that I'd seen these emotions many times before. I placed my hand on his.

"Do you understand?" he said. "You can find the sums of all the natural numbers."

"I understand."

"Just by lining up the dots in a triangle. That's all there is to it."

"Yes, I see that now."

"But do you really understand?"

"Don't worry," I told him. "Everything's going to be all right. How can you cry, look at these beautiful triangular numbers."

Just then the door to the examination room opened and Root emerged.

"See!" he said, giving his bandaged hand a wave. "I'm fine."

Leaving the clinic, we suddenly realized that we were starving, so we decided to eat out. Since the Professor hated crowds, we went to the emptiest restaurant in the arcade near the station and had a bowl of curry and rice. There were almost no other customers, so we might have guessed that the curry wouldn't be particularly good; but Root, who almost never ate out, was delighted. He also seemed pleased to have such a dramatic bandage (for a relatively minor injury), as if he were the hero of some great battle.

"I won't be able to help with the dishes or even take a bath for a while," he said, a bit full of himself.

The Professor carried him home on his back, and Root was less worried about being seen now that it was dark. Perhaps he was just being considerate of the Professor. Whatever the reason, he climbed on without objection and rode happily. A thin sliver of moon hung above the row of sycamores glowing under the street lamps. A pleasant breeze was blowing, our stomachs were full, and Root's hand would heal. I felt a great sense of contentment. My footsteps fell in with the Professor's, and Root's tennis shoes swung back and forth in time.

After seeing the Professor home, we headed back to our apartment. For some reason Root was suddenly in a bad mood. He went straight to his room and turned on the radio, and refused to answer when I called to tell him to take off his bloodstained clothes.

"Are the Tigers losing?" I asked. He was standing at his desk, glaring at the radio. They were playing the Giants. "They lost yesterday, didn't they?" Still no answer. The announcer informed us that the score was tied 2-2 in the bottom of the ninth, with Nakata and Kuwata locked in a pitchers' duel. "Does it hurt?" I asked. He bit his lip and kept his eyes on the radio. "If it hurts, take the medicine the doctor gave us. I'll get you some water."

"No," he said.

"You really should," I coaxed. "You don't want it to get infected."

"I said it doesn't hurt."

He clenched his bandaged fist and rapped it against the desk, using his good hand to hide the tears welling up in his eyes. This clearly had nothing to do with the Tigers.

"Why are you doing that?" I said. "They just finished stitching you up. What am I supposed to do if you start bleeding again?"

Tears streamed down his cheeks now. I tried to check whether blood was soaking through the bandage, but he brushed my hand away. Cheers erupted from the radio—a two out single.

"Are you mad because I went out and left you with the Professor? Or are you embarrassed because you couldn't handle the knife? Or because you made a mistake in front of the Professor?" He'd fallen silent again. Kameyama was up at bat.

"*Kuwata has been nearly unhittable. . . . He's struck out his last two at bats . . . will it be another fastball? . . . Here's the windup. . . .*"

The cheers rose again and again, drowning out the announcer, but Root seemed indifferent. He sat perfectly still as the tears continued to roll down his cheeks.

I realized I had seen two men cry this evening. I had, of course, seen Root's tears countless times before—as an infant, when he'd wanted to be held or fed; and later, during tantrums, or when he lost his grandmother. And, for that matter, at the moment he came into this world. But these tears were different, and no matter how I tried to wipe them away, they seemed to flow from a place I could never reach.

"Are you mad because the Professor couldn't dress the wound properly?" I asked at last.

"No," said Root. He stared at me for a moment and then he spoke so calmly it seemed as though he had completely regained control of himself. "I'm mad because you didn't trust him. I'll never forgive you for that."

Kameyama hit the second pitch into right center, and Wada scored from first to end the game. The announcer was shouting and the roar of the crowd swept over us.

The next day, the Professor and I recopied his note tags. "I wonder where all this blood came from," he said, checking himself for a cut.

"Root, my son, hurt his hand with a knife—but it wasn't serious."

"Your son? That's terrible! It looks like it bled all over."

"No, he's just fine, thanks to you."

"Really? I helped?"

"Of course. How do you think the blood got on you?"

I pulled the notes from his suit one by one. Most were covered with an incomprehensible scrawl of math symbols—as though few things other than numbers were worth remembering.

"And when you finished helping Root, you taught me something important in the waiting room."

"Something important?"

"You taught me about triangular numbers, and the formula for finding the sum of the natural numbers from 1 to 10—something I could never have imagined, something sublime." I held out the most important note. "Shall we start with this one?"

The Professor copied out a new tag and read it quietly to himself.

"My memory lasts only eighty minutes."

5

I'm not sure if they were related to his mathematical abilities, but the Professor had some pretty peculiar talents. For instance, he could instantly reverse the syllables in a phrase and repeat them backward. We discovered this one day when Root was struggling to come up with palindromes for a homework assignment in Japanese.

"It doesn't make any sense, but it's the same forward and backward: 'A nut for a jar of tuna'—what's that supposed to mean? Nobody would trade a jar of tuna for a nut."

"Nut a for natu of jar a trade would dybono," the Professor murmured.

"What did you say, Professor?" Root asked.

"Sorfespro, say you did what?"

"What are you doing?"

"Ingdo you are what?" said the Professor.

"Mom, I think he's gone crazy," Root said.

"We'd all be crazy if we said things backward." The Professor sounded a bit sheepish. I asked him how he did it, but he didn't seem to know. He hadn't practiced, he did it almost without thinking, and had assumed long ago that it was something anybody could do.

"Don't be ridiculous," I told him. "I couldn't reverse syllables in my head like that. You could be in the *Guinness Book,* or on one of those TV shows."

The prospect of being on TV seemed to alarm the Professor; and yet, this trick came to him with even greater ease when he was anxious. One thing seemed clear, however: he was not reading the reversed syllables from a picture in his head. It was more a matter of rhythm, and once his ear had caught it, he instinctively flipped the syllables around.

"It's like solving a problem in mathematics," he said. "The formula doesn't just come floating into your head in finished form. It starts as a vague outline and then gradually becomes clearer. It's a bit like that."

"Can you do it again?" Root said, forgetting his homework. He was completely fascinated by the Professor's ability. "Let's see. Try Hanshin Tigers."

"Gersti shinhan."

"Radio calisthenics."

"Icsthenisca odira."

"The cafeteria had fried chicken today."

"Dayto enchick fried had riateecaf the."

"Amieable numbers."

"Bersnum blecaiam."

"I drew an armadillo at the zoo."

"Zoo the at lodilmaar an drew I."

Root and I tossed out sentences for the Professor one after another, challenging him with longer and tougher ones. At first, Root wrote out each one and checked it, but the Professor's performance was flawless, and Root eventually gave up. We simply said something—anything at all—and the Professor spoke it back to us in reverse syllables, without a second's hesitation.

"Unbelievable! It's awesome, Professor! You should show people. You should be proud. How come we didn't know after all this time?"

"I'm not sure what you mean," said the Professor. "What is there to be proud of?"

"But you *should* be proud! It's amazing! People would love to see this!"

"Thank you," said the Professor, looking down bashfully. He placed his hand on Root's flat head—a head oddly suited to supporting a hand. "This skill of mine is completely useless. Who needs a lot of scrambled-up words? But I'm glad you find it interesting."

The Professor thought of a palindrome for Root's assignment:

"I prefer pi."

The Professor had another talent: finding the first sign of the evening star in the afternoon sky.

"Ah!" he said one day from his easy chair, when the sun was

still high up in the sky. Thinking he was talking in his sleep or muttering something to himself, I didn't answer. "Ah!" he said again, and pointed with one unsteady finger out the window. "The evening star."

He was not speaking to me, but to himself. I stopped what I was doing in the kitchen to look where he was pointing—though I couldn't see anything but the sky. Perhaps too many numbers are causing hallucinations, I wondered; but, as though he'd read my mind, he pointed once again. "Look, there it is."

His finger was wrinkled and cracked, and there was dirt under the nail. I blinked and tried to focus, but I couldn't see anything but a few wisps of cloud.

"It's a little early for stars," I said as gently as I could.

"The evening star means night is coming," he said, as if I'd never said a word. Then he lowered his arm and nodded off again.

I don't know what the evening star meant to him, perhaps finding it in the sky soothed his nerves, or maybe it was simply a habit. And I don't know how he could see it so long before anyone else—he barely noticed the food I set right in front of him. For whatever reason, he would point his withered finger at a single spot in the vast sky—always the right place, as I eventually discovered—and that spot had significance for him and no one else.

Root's cut healed, but his attitude was slower to recover. He behaved himself when we were with the Professor, but when it was just the two of us, he became moody and short. One day, when his clean, white bandage had begun to look dingy, I sat down in front of him and bowed my head.

"I'm sorry," I said. "It was wrong of me to doubt the Professor, even for a moment. I'm sorry and I apologize."

I thought he might ignore me, but he turned and looked at me with a very serious expression. He sat up straight, picking at the end of his bandage.

"All right, I accept. But I'll never forget what happened." And at that, we shook hands.

It was only two stitches, but even after he'd grown up, he still had the scar between his thumb and forefinger—proof of how much the Professor had cared about him.

One day while I was straightening the shelves in the Professor's study I came across a cookie tin buried under a pile of mathematics books. I gingerly pulled off the rusted lid, thinking I'd find moldy sweets, but, to my surprise, the box was filled with baseball cards.

There were hundreds of them, packed tightly into the large tin, and it was clear that the collection had been treasured by its owner. The cards were spotless, protected from fingerprints and dirt in individual cellophane wrappers. Not one was out of place nor was there a single bent corner or crease. Hand-lettered dividers labeled the players by position—"Pitchers," "Second Basemen," "Left Fielders"—and each section was in alphabetical order. And to a man, they were all Hanshin Tigers. They were perfectly preserved, but the pictures and player bios on them were quite old. Most of the photos were in black and white, and while I could follow a few of the references—"Yoshio Yoshida, the modern-day Mercury," or "the Zatopekesque pitching of Minoru Maruyama"—I was lost when it came to the "diabolic rainbow ball of Tadashi Wakabayashi," or "the incomparable Sho Kageura."

One player had been given special treatment: Yutaka Enatsu. Instead of being filed by position, he had a separate section all to himself. While the other cards were covered in cellophane, Enatsu's were protected by stiff plastic sheaths.

There were numerous Enatsu cards, depicting him in various poses, but this was not the potbellied Enatsu I knew. In these cards he was trim and young and, of course, wearing the uniform of the Hanshin Tigers.

Born May 15, 1948, in Nara Prefecture. Throws left, bats left. h:179cm. w:90kg. Graduated Osaka Gakuin High School, 1967; drafted 1st by Hanshin. Following year, broke Sandy Koufax's record (382) for most strikeouts in a Major League season with 401. Struck out 9 consecutive batters in the 1971 All-Star Game (Nishinomiya), 8 failed to make contact. 1973 season, pitched no-hitter. "The Lofty Lefty." "Super Southpaw."

Enatsu's player profile and statistics appeared on the backs of the cards in tiny print. Here he was, glove on his knee, reading the signals. Or in full windup. Or again, at the end of the pitch, eyes boring into the catcher's mitt. Enatsu on the mound, his fierce stance like a Deva King guarding a temple. And always on his uniform, the perfect number 28.

I returned the cards to the box and pressed the lid down as carefully as I'd taken it off.

Hidden farther back behind the shelves, I found a stack of dusty notebooks. Judging from the discoloration of the paper and ink, they were nearly as old as the baseball cards. Long years of pressure from the tightly packed books had loosened the string holding the thirty or so folders together, and the covers were warped and bent.

I flipped through page after page, but I found no Japanese—just numbers, symbols, and letters of the alphabet. Mysterious geometric forms were followed by equally strange curves and graphs, all the Professor's work. The handwriting was younger and more vigorous, but the ribbonlike fours and the slanted fives were unmistakable.

There is nothing more shameful for a housekeeper than to rummage through her employer's personal property. But the exquisite beauty of the notebooks made me oblivious. The formulas snaked across the pages by some logic of their own, ignoring the lines on the paper; and just when they seemed to resolve into a kind of order, they would divide again into apparently random strands. They were punctuated with arrows and $\sqrt{}$ and Σ and all sorts of other symbols, they covered the paper with dark blotches in some places, and traced faintly like delicate insect tracks in others.

Needless to say, I could not understand any of the mysteries concealed in the notebooks. Yet somehow, I wanted to stay there forever, just staring at the formulas. Was the proof of the Artin conjecture that the Professor had spoken of somewhere here? And certainly there must be some of his work on the beloved prime numbers . . . and perhaps the notes for the thesis that had won Prize No. 284 were here as well. In my own way, I could sense all kinds of things from the mysterious numbers and figures—the passion in a pencil smudge, the impatience of a crossed-out mistake, the certitude in a passage underscored with two thick lines. This glimpse into the Professor's world thrilled me deeply.

As I looked more closely, I began to notice scribbles here and there in the margins that even I could read: "Define terms of solution more carefully." "Invalid when only partially stable." "New approach, useless." "Will it be in time?" "14:00 with N, in front of the library."

Though these notes were simply scrawled in the spaces between the calculations, the handwriting here seemed much more purposeful than the scribbled notes attached to the Professor's suit. In these pages, the Professor had walked beyond beaten paths, looking for truth in a place no one knows.

What had happened in front of the library at two o'clock? And who was N? I found myself hoping that the meeting had been a happy one for the professor.

I ran my fingers over the lines of the formula, a long chain of numbers and symbols that flowed from one page to the next. As I followed the chain, link by link, the room faded and I found myself in a dark, silent place of numbers. But I felt no fear, certain in the knowledge that the Professor would guide me toward eternal, unchangeable truths.

As I turned the last page of the last notebook, the chain abruptly broke, and I was left in the shadows. If I could have read on just a little further, I might have found what I was looking for; but the chain simply slipped from my fingers and I would never grasp its end.

"Excuse me," the Professor called from the bathroom. "I'm sorry to bother you when you're busy. . . ."

I quickly put everything back in its place. "Coming," I called, as brightly as I could.

In May, I bought three tickets for the Tigers game against Hiroshima on June 2. The Tigers played only twice a season in the town where we lived and, if you let the chance go by, it was a long wait until the next game.

Root had never been to a ball game. In fact, with the exception of a trip to the zoo with his grandmother, he had never been to a museum or a movie theater or anywhere at all. From the time he was born, I had been obsessed with making ends meet, and somehow I had forgotten to make time to have fun with my son.

When I'd found the baseball cards in the cookie tin, it had suddenly occurred to me that a baseball game might be just the thing for a disabled old man who passed his days wandering in the world of numbers and a boy who had spent nearly every day of his life waiting for his mother to come home from work.

The price of three reserved seats on the third baseline was a bit more than I could afford—especially since I'd just had the unexpected expense of our visit to the clinic. But there would be plenty of time to worry about money later; who knew when the old man and the boy would have a chance to enjoy a ball game together. Besides, the Professor had only known baseball through his cards; if I could show him the real thing—the sweat-soaked pinstripes, the home-run ball vanishing into a sea of cheers, the cleat-scarred pitcher's mound—that would be a privilege. Even if I wouldn't be able to produce Enatsu.

I thought it was a wonderful idea, but Root's reaction surprised me: "He probably won't want to go," he muttered. "The Professor hates crowds." He had a point. I'd had trouble convincing the Professor to go to the barbershop; and a baseball game was the antithesis of his beloved peace and quiet. "And how are you going to get him ready? He can't think about it ahead of time." Root always showed amazing insight when it came to the Professor. "Everything's a surprise for him. He can't plan ahead, and if you spring something big on him out of the blue like this, he could die of shock."

"Don't be ridiculous," I said. "What if we pin the ticket to his suit?"

"I don't think it'd work," Root said, shaking his head. "Have you ever seen him remember anything from all those notes?"

"Well, he checks my picture on his sleeve every morning when I arrive."

"But he couldn't even tell the difference between you and me from that terrible drawing."

"He's a math genius, not an artist."

"Every time I see the Professor writing a note with that little pencil, I feel like crying," Root said.

"Why?"

"Because it's sad!" he said. He was almost angry now. I just nodded, unwilling to argue further. "And there's one more problem," he added, in a resigned tone of voice. "None of the players he knew are still on the Tigers. They all retired."

He was right again. If the players on his cards did not appear in the game, he would be confused and disappointed. Even the team uniform had changed since his day. The baseball stadium itself was bound to upset the Professor as well—with the fans drinking and shouting and screaming, it was the very opposite of a tranquil mathematical theorem. Root's fears were all justified.

"I see what you mean, but I've already bought the tickets. Forget about the Professor for a moment; would you like to see the Tigers play?"

He looked down for a moment, perhaps trying to preserve his dignity, but he soon began to squirm and finally, unable to contain himself, he danced all around me.

"Yes!" he shouted. "More than anything!" He danced and danced and then hung on my neck. "Thank you!" he said.

It was rainy season, and we'd been worried about the weather, but June 2 dawned bright and sunny. We set out on the four-fifty bus, while there was still a good bit of light in the sky. Some of the other passengers seemed to be heading to the game as well.

Root carried a plastic megaphone he had borrowed from a friend, and, of course, he wore his Tigers cap. Every ten minutes or so, he asked me if I'd remembered the tickets. I was carrying a basket of sandwiches in one hand and a Thermos of tea in the other; but his constant questions made me uneasy, and I found myself slipping my hand into the pocket of my skirt just to be sure.

The Professor was dressed as always: a suit covered with notes, moldy shoes, pencils in his breast pocket.

I'd told him about the baseball game at three thirty, exactly eighty minutes before the bus was due to depart. Root had already arrived from school, and we tried to bring up the game as casually as possible. At first, the Professor didn't understand what we were saying. I don't think he was even aware that professional baseball was played at stadiums all over the country and that anyone who wanted to could buy a ticket and go to a game—not that this was especially odd, since he had only recently learned that you could listen to a game on the radio. Until now, baseball had only existed in the form of statistics and as illustrated cards.

"You want me to go?" he asked, sounding apprehensive.

"You certainly don't have to if you don't want. But we'd like you to come with us."

"To the stadium . . . on a bus?" Thinking about things was the Professor's special talent, and if we'd left him alone, he might have considered the matter until long after the game had ended. "And will we see Enatsu?" He'd struck us where we were most vulnerable, but Root gave the answer we'd agreed on.

"Unfortunately, he played against the Giants at Koshien the day before yesterday, so he won't be pitching today. I'm sorry, Professor."

"You don't have to apologize. But it is a shame. . . . Did he win the other day at least?"

"Sure he did. His seventh win of the season."

At the time, in 1992, the pitcher who wore number 28, Yoshihiro Nakada, played only rarely due to a shoulder injury. It was hard to know whether it was lucky or unlucky that no one in the dugout would be wearing number 28. If the player wearing Enatsu's number wasn't a pitcher, the Professor would have realized something was wrong, but if he had seen number 28 throwing in the bullpen, perhaps he wouldn't be able to tell the difference. He'd never seen Enatsu play, so he wouldn't recognize his windup. But if the Tigers decided to play Nakada, there would have been no mistaking him from the mound and the Professor's shock could have been terrible. Nakada was not even a lefty, like Enatsu. It would have been easier all around if there were no 28 at all.

"Let's go!" Root urged. "It'll be more fun if you come, too." And that was enough—the Professor decided to go.

He sat gripping the arms of his seat all the way to the stadium, just as he had at the barbershop. When we had to get off the bus he let go of the armrest and held tightly to Root's hand. We were mostly silent as we walked through the grounds to the stadium and stood in the crowded passageway leading to our seats. The Professor was no doubt shocked to find himself in a place so utterly different from his usual surroundings, and Root was overcome with excitement at the prospect of seeing his beloved Tigers. They both seemed to have lost the power of speech and merely stared around in awe.

"Is everything okay?" I asked from time to time, and the Professor would nod and grip Root's hand tightly.

As we reached the top of the stairs that led to the seats above third base, all three of us let out a cry. The diamond in all its grandeur was laid out before us—the soft, dark earth of the infield, the spotless bases, the straight white lines, and the manicured grass. The evening sky seemed so close you could touch it, and at that moment, as if they had been awaiting our arrival, the lights came on. The stadium looked like a spaceship descended from the heavens.

Did the Professor enjoy the game? Later, when Root and I spoke of that remarkable day, we were never sure. And there was always a part of us that regretted putting this good-natured old man through such an ordeal.

But those moments we shared, the sights and sounds of the game, haven't faded with the years. If anything, they seem brighter and more vivid as time goes by, indelibly etched in our minds. The cracked, uncomfortable seats, the egg salad sandwiches with too much mustard, the lights of a plane that cut across the sky above the stadium like a shooting star. We remember every detail, and when we talk about that night, we're able to conjure up and bring back the Professor, as if he were sitting right beside us.

Our favorite part was the Professor's crush on the girl who was selling drinks in the stands. The Tigers had just finished their half of the second inning, and Root, who had already eaten his sandwich, announced that he wanted some juice. I was about to flag down a vendor when the Professor stopped me with a quiet but emphatic "No." When I asked him what was wrong, he refused to answer, but when I started to wave to the next girl, he spoke up again. "No!" For some reason, he seemed to disapprove of Root having a juice.

"Just make do with the tea I brought from home," I told Root.

"I don't want that. It's bitter."

"Then I'll go get you some milk at the concession stand."

"I'm not a baby! And they don't sell milk here. At a baseball game, you're supposed to have juice in a big paper cup—that's the rule." It was typical of Root to have an ideal vision of how things were supposed to be. I turned back to the Professor.

"Don't you think we could let him have just one?"

His expression was still grave as he brought his mouth close to my ear and whispered, "Get it from that girl over there." He pointed to a young woman who was climbing the other aisle.

"Why?" I asked.

At first he refused to explain, but Root's pestering finally wore him down. "Because she's the prettiest," he said simply.

Indeed, the Professor had a good eye. She was by far the most beautiful girl, and she had the sweetest smile. Finally, the girl in question arrived at the row directly below ours, and the Professor called out to get her attention. The fact that his hand was shaking as he passed her the money or that his suit was covered with scraps of paper didn't seem to faze her, and she continued to smile pleasantly as she handed him the juice. Root had complained about how long it had taken to get his drink, but his mood improved when the Professor bought him popcorn, ice cream, and a second juice when the girl came by again. We were so busy scanning the stands for the pretty young vendor and buying treats for Root that we missed the Tigers taking the lead with four hits in the top of the third.

This unexpected distraction aside, the Professor was still a mathematician at heart. As he sat down and looked around at the stadium, the first words out his mouth were: "The diamond is 27.43 meters on each side." And when he noticed that his seat number was 714 and Root's was 715, he began to lecture again and completely forgot to sit down.

"The home run record Babe Ruth set in 1935 is 714. On April 8, 1974, Hank Aaron broke that record, hitting his 715th off of Al Downing of the Dodgers. The product of 714 and 715 is equal to the product of the first seven prime numbers: $714 \times 715 = 2 \times 3 \times 5 \times 7 \times 11 \times 13 \times 17 = 510510$. And, the sum of the prime factors of 714 equals the sum of the prime factors of 715: $714 = 2 \times 3 \times 7 \times 17$; $715 = 5 \times 11 \times 13$; $2 + 3 + 7 + 17 = 5 + 11 + 13 = 29$. A pair of consecutive whole numbers with these properties is quite rare. There are only 26 such pairs up to 20,000. This one is the Ruth-Aaron pair. Just like prime numbers, they are more rare as the numbers get larger. And 5 and 6 are the smallest pair. But the proof to show that those pairs are infinite in number is quite difficult. . . . The important thing is that I'm sitting in 714 and you're in 715, instead of the opposite. It's the young who have to break the old records. That's the way the world works, don't you think?"

"That's great, Professor. But look, there's Tsuyoshi Shinjo!"

Root always listened carefully to these speeches, but he showed little interest in the significance of his seat number.

The Professor talked about numbers throughout the game—just as he always did when he was nervous. His voice grew louder and louder with each inning; he would not be drowned out by the crowd.

The starting pitcher, Nakagomi, was greeted with a tremendous cheer as he was announced and headed out to the mound. At the same moment, the Professor said, "The height of the mound is 10 inches, or 25.4 centimeters. The infield slopes at a rate of one inch per foot for the first six feet toward the plate."

He noticed that the first seven men in the order for Hiroshima hit left-handed: "Left-handed hitters against left-handed pitchers have a cumulative batting average of .2568. Right-handed hitters hit .2649 against right-handed pitchers." Or, when Nishida, on the Hiroshima team, stole a base and the crowd booed: "It takes 0.8 seconds from the time the pitcher begins his windup to the time he releases the ball. In this case, the pitch was a curveball that took 0.6 seconds to reach the catcher's mitt, and then 2 full seconds for the catcher to throw it to second base, which means the runner had 3.4 seconds total to run the 24 meters from first to second base without being thrown out, running at more than 7 meters per second, or 25.2 kilometers per hour."

Fortunately, his commentary did not cause us any trouble, since the group to our left politely ignored him, while the man sitting to our right was amused. He helped us to keep the Professor calm.

"You seem to know a lot more about it than that lousy announcer," he said. "You'd make a great scorekeeper. Why don't you figure out how the Tigers can win the pennant?" When he wasn't cheering for the players on the field, he appeared to listen carefully to everything the Professor said, even though I doubt he could understand it. Thanks to this kind man, the Professor's mathematical commentary moved beyond the level of farce and, in some sense, revealed a kind of logic to the game. For that, the man shared his peanuts with us.

The Tigers held their lead through the fifth inning on hits from Wada and Kuji. The sun had gone down and the evening grew chilly, so I made Root put on his jacket and I handed the Professor his lap robe; then I was busy wiping everyone's hands before we ate, and by the time we were properly settled, I was amazed to see that two more runs had been scored. Root, beside himself with happiness, was screaming through his megaphone, while the Professor, resting his sandwich on his lap, applauded awkwardly.

He had become completely absorbed in the game. The angle of the ball flying off the bat would leave him marveling, squinting at the field and nodding. From time to time he would peek into the picnic basket of the people sitting in front of us, or glance up at the moon shining between the branches of the poplars just outside the stadium.

Hanshin fans seemed to dominate the stands behind third base. The area was blanketed in yellow jerseys, and the cheers for the Tigers were loud and long. Even if the Hiroshima supporters had wanted to answer, they had little to cheer about as Nakagomi struck out one batter after another.

The Tigers fans roared each time Nakagomi threw a strike; and when a run came in, the stadium erupted. I had never in my entire life seen so many people united in celebration. Even the Professor looked positively elated—and here was a man who only seemed to have two facial expressions, the one he wore when he was thinking and the one he gave me when I interrupted those thoughts. You might even say that he, too, had been transported by the cheers.

But the prize for the most original way of expressing enthusiasm went to the Kameyama fan clinging to the wire fence of the backstop. In his early twenties, he wore a Kameyama jersey over his work clothes and had a transistor radio clipped to his belt. His fingers were wrapped tight around the backstop and he hung there throughout the game. When Kameyama was out in left field, the young man's eyes never left him, and when he appeared in the on-deck circle, he grew agitated. When Kameyama was up at bat, he called out his name in one continuous chant that went from joy to despair. In order to get a few millimeters closer to his hero, he had pressed his face against the fence, so that the mesh pattern had become imprinted on his forehead. He wasted no energy booing the other team, nor did he complain when the great man himself struck out. Instead, he poured his whole heart and soul into repeating that one word: Kameyama.

As we watched him, we began to wonder what would happen if Kameyama actually got a hit; and when, in the middle of the fourth inning, he knocked it into left field, the spectators sitting behind him reached up out of their seats, as if expecting him to faint dead away. Kameyama's ball shot between second and third and bounced into the outfield. It glowed white against the grass, and the outfielders scurried after it. The young man screamed for a long time, and even after his lungs were empty, he sobbed faintly and writhed against the fence. Paciorek was up next, and this ecstatic display continued well into his warm-up. By comparison, the Professor's reaction to the game was reserved and respectful.

He didn't seem to care that none of the players were familiar from the cards he had collected. Perhaps he was so busy trying to connect the rules and statistics stored in his head with the game on the field that he forgot to worry about the names of the players.

"What's in that little bag?" he asked Root.

"That's the rosin bag. It has pine tar to keep their hands from slipping."

"And why does the catcher keeping running toward first base like that?"

"He's backing up the throw, in case it gets away from the first baseman."

"But it looks like some fans are sitting in the dugout. . . ."

"I think those are the interpreters for the foreign players."

The Professor turned to Root with his questions. He could tell you the kinetic energy of a pitch traveling 150 kph or the relationship between ball temperature and the distance a hit would travel, but he had no idea what a rosin bag was. He had loosened his grip on Root's hand, but he still kept close and relied on him for reassurance. He talked throughout the game. From time to time he bought something from the pretty woman selling concessions, or ate a few peanuts. But he never stopped glancing over in the direction of the bullpen, hoping to catch a glimpse of number 28.

The Tigers took a 6-0 lead going into the seventh inning, and the game seemed to be moving along quickly. But all attention soon shifted from the game itself to Nakagomi, who by the final inning was pitching a no-hitter.

Though their team had been ahead all along, the mood among the Tigers fans behind third base had grown more tense with each pitch. As the Tigers' last batter struck out and they took to the field, murmurs and moans could be heard from here and there in the bleachers. If the team had continued to rack up runs, it might have been easier to bear, but they had not scored since the fifth inning and there was no change on the scoreboard. Like it or not, the game was an intense duel and we were all focused on Nakagomi.

As he headed for the mound in the bottom of the ninth, someone in the stands finally gave voice to the thought that was on everyone's mind: "Three more outs!" A murmur of disapproval went through the bleachers, as though this encouragement was the surest way to jinx the no-hitter; but the only comment came from the Professor:

"The odds of pitching a no-hitter are 0.18 percent."

Hiroshima sent in a pinch hitter for the leadoff batter. No one had ever heard of him, but no one was paying attention anyway. Nakagomi threw his first pitch.

The ball cracked off the bat and sailed into the midnight blue sky, tracing a graceful parabola. It was whiter than the moon, more beautiful than the stars. Every eye was focused on that one point; but at the instant the ball reached its apogee and began to fall, the elegant arc vanished and it became a meteorite, hurtling toward us in a blinding streak.

"Watch out!" the Professor cried in my ear. The ball grazed Root's shoulder, struck the concrete floor, and bounded off behind us. I turned to find the Professor with his arms spread out to cover Root, shielding him with his entire body to keep him from harm.

Even after the ball had rolled to a stop, the Professor remained frozen for some time, with Root pinned beneath him.

"Please watch out for foul balls," the stadium announcer reminded us.

"It's okay now," I whispered. Peanut shells scattered down from the Professor's hand.

"A baseball weighing 141.7 grams . . . falling from a height of

15 meters . . . an iron ball weighing 12.1 kilograms . . . the force is 85.39 times. . . ." the Professor whispered his incantation, huddling over seats 714 and 715. My son and the Professor shared a secret bond now that no one could break, just as the Professor and I were linked by 220 and 284.

A cry went up in the stadium. Nakagomi's second pitch had been hit into right field, and we watched as it rolled across the turf.

"Kameyama!" the man at the fence cried one last time.

6

It was nearly ten o'clock when we reached the Professor's cottage. Root was still excited, but he was now fighting back yawns. I had intended to see the Professor home and then head to our apartment, but he seemed so exhausted that I decided we should stay until he was safely in bed.

Perhaps the crowded bus on the way home had been too much for him. He had almost panicked as the waves of people swayed against him, obviously terrified that they would tear off his tags. "We're almost there," I'd told him again and again. But he gave no sign that he heard, and he twisted and squirmed the whole way home in an effort to avoid being touched.

He hastily undressed, which I suspect was his habit. He threw his socks, coat, tie, and trousers on the floor, and slipped into bed in his underwear without brushing his teeth. I pretended to myself that he had brushed them very quickly when he'd disappeared into the bathroom.

"Thank you," he said before he closed his eyes. "It was great fun."

"Even though he blew the no-hitter," said Root, kneeling by the bed to straighten the Professor's quilt.

"Enatsu threw a no-hitter," murmured the Professor. "That one went to extra innings. It was on August 30, 1973, and the Tigers were battling the Giants for the pennant right up to the last game of the season. They were playing the Chunichi Dragons, and Enatsu himself hit a walk-off home run in the bottom of the eleventh to win the game 1 to 0. He did it all himself—offense and defense. But he wasn't pitching today, was he?"

"No, we'll have to check the rotation next time before we get tickets," said Root.

"But they won," I added.

"That's right," said the Professor. "A fine score, 6 to 1."

"They moved up to second place, and the Giants lost to Taiyo, so they're in the cellar. It doesn't get much better than that, does it, Professor?"

"No, it doesn't. But the best part was going to the game with you. Now listen to your mother and get home and go right to bed. You've got school tomorrow." He smiled faintly, but his eyes closed even before Root could answer. His eyelids were red, his lips were cracked, and he had begun to perspire. I felt his fore-head and realized he had a high fever.

I hesitated a moment, but soon decided that Root and I would have to stay the night with him. I could never ignore a sick person, much less the Professor. Rather than worry about the terms of my contract or the agency rules, it was easier simply to stay and take care of him.

Not surprisingly, a search of the house failed to turn up any-thing that might be useful for treating a fever—no ice pack, ther-mometer, gargle, or medicines. I peeked out the window and saw a light still on in the main house, and for a split second I thought I saw a shadowy figure standing near the hedge. It occurred to me that I could use some help from the Professor's sister-in-law, but then I remembered my promise not to involve her in any diffi-culties that might occur in the cottage. I drew the curtains.

Realizing that I would have to manage for myself, I crushed some ice into a plastic bag, wrapped it in a towel, and set about trying to cool the Professor's neck and back. Then I covered him in a heavy winter blanket and made tea to hydrate him. This was my usual routine when Root had a fever.

I put Root to bed on the sofa in the corner of the study. It had been covered with books, but when I cleared them away it proved to be comfortable enough. Root was still worried about the Pro-fessor, but he fell asleep almost immediately, his Tigers cap perched on a stack of math books.

"How are you feeling?" I asked the Professor. "Are you in pain? Are you thirsty?" He did not reply, and as he was sleeping soundly I assumed the fever would pass. His breathing was a little irregular, but there was no sign that he was in any pain. He looked almost peaceful. Even when I changed the ice packs or wiped down his damp arms and legs, he remained limp and did not open his eyes.

Out of his note-covered suit, his body was surprisingly thin and frail. His skin was pale and soft, the flesh on his arms and thighs and belly was wrinkled and slack. His fingernails seemed old and tired. I remembered something the Professor had told me, something a mathematician with a difficult name once said: "Math has proven the existence of God, because it is absolute and without contradiction; but the devil must exist as well, because we cannot prove it." The Professor's body had been consumed by the devil of mathematics.

As the night wore on, his fever seemed to worsen. His breath was hot, sweat poured off him, and the ice packs melted quickly. I began to worry—should I run out to the drugstore? Was it wrong to have forced him to go to the game? Would the fever do more damage to his brain? Eventually I consoled myself with the thought that he was sleeping peacefully, and I decided everything would be all right.

I wrapped myself in the lap robe that we'd taken along to the stadium and lay down by the bed. Moonlight shone in through a crack in the curtains. The game seemed a distant memory. The Professor was asleep to my left, Root to my right. When I closed my eyes, the world was filled with sound. The Professor's soft snoring, the drip of melting ice, Root muttering in his sleep, the creak of the sofa. The sounds comforted me, allowing me to forget about the Professor's crisis, as I drifted off to sleep.

The next morning, before the Professor woke up, Root left for school. He took the Tigers megaphone to return to his friend and promised to stop at the apartment to collect his books. When I went to check on the Professor, he was still in a deep sleep, but he seemed less flushed and his breathing was steady and calm. I began to worry that he had been asleep for too long. I gently touched his forehead and rolled back the blanket. I tried tickling him on the neck and chest and under his arms. I even tried blowing in his ear. But there was no response, other than a slight twitching of his eyes under their heavy lids.

Around noon, as I was working in the kitchen, I heard a noise from the study, and when I went to see, he was sitting on the edge of the bed dressed in his usual suit, his chin drooping down on his chest.

"You shouldn't be up," I told him. "You have a fever and you need to rest." He looked at me for a moment without saying anything and then looked down again. His eyes were full of sleep, his hair was wild, and his tie was badly askew. "Let's get you out of that suit and into some clean underwear. You were all sweaty last night. I'll go and buy you some pajamas later. You'll feel better when we get you fixed up and change the sheets. You were exhausted—from the long ball game. I'm sorry we tired you out, but I think you'll be fine now. If we keep you warm in bed and properly fed, you'll be as good as new in no time. That always works when Root has a fever. . . . So, let's start by getting something in your stomach. Would you like some apple juice?"

Before I'd finished, he pushed me away and turned his back; and as he did, I realized I had made the most basic mistake: he no longer remembered the baseball game, or even who I was. He sat on the bed staring down at his lap, his back more hunched over than it had been the day before. His tired body remained still, his mind wandered in a fog. All passion had deserted him, and even the affection he showed toward Root was gone.

A moment later, I realized he was sobbing quietly. At first, I couldn't tell where the sound was coming from him—it sounded like the stuttering of a broken music box. These sobs were very different from the ones he'd cried when Root cut his hand; they were private, desolate, and for no one other than himself.

The Professor was reading the note clipped in the most prominent spot on his jacket, the one he could never avoid seeing as he got dressed. "My memory lasts only eighty minutes." I sat down on the edge of the bed, unsure whether there was anything more I could do for him. My mistake had been the simplest one—and perhaps the most fatal. Every morning, when the Professor woke up, a note in his own hand reminded him of his affliction, and that the dreams he'd dreamed were not last night's but those of some night in the distant past back when his memory had ended—it was as though yesterday had never happened. The Professor who had shielded Root from the foul ball last night was gone. Somehow, I had never quite understood what it meant for him to wake up alone each morning to this cruel revelation.

"I'm your housekeeper," I said, when the sobs had subsided for a moment. "I'm here to help you." He looked up at me through his tears. "My son will come this evening. We call him Root, because his head is flat. You gave him that name." I pointed to the picture of me on his jacket, grateful it had survived the bus ride home from the ballpark.

"When is your birthday?" he said. His voice was weak from the fever, but I was relieved to hear a sound other than sobbing.

"February twentieth," I said. "It's an amicable number, 220, good friends with 284."

• • • •

His fever lasted three days, and he slept nearly the whole time. He didn't wake up for meals or show any interest in the snacks I left by his bed, so finally I was forced to feed him bite by bite. I would prop him up in bed and pinch his cheeks, and when he opened his mouth, I was ready with the spoon. He could barely stay awake for a full cup of soup, nodding off before I'd managed to feed half of it to him.

In the end, he recovered without seeing a doctor. Since going out had caused his fever in the first place, I felt that the best thing was to keep him at home in a peaceful place. Besides, it would have been all but impossible to get him up and dressed and out to the clinic.

When Root arrived from school, he would go straight to the study and stand by the Professor's bed, watching him sleep until I told him he had to do his homework.

On the morning of the fourth day, the fever finally broke, and he soon made a quick recovery. He started sleeping less, and his appetite returned. Soon, he was well enough to sit at the dinner table, and then to tie his own tie; and before long he was back in his easy chair reading his math books. He even resumed working on his puzzles. I knew he was fully recovered when he began scolding me for interrupting his work, and when he started greeting Root at the door again with a hug. They took up their math drills, the Professor rubbed Root's head—everything was normal again.

Not long after the Professor had recovered, I received a message summoning me to the office of the Director of the Akebono

Housekeeping Agency. It was a bad sign to be called in when it wasn't time for a regular performance review. It could mean that a client had complained and you were going to be reprimanded, or that someone was demanding a formal apology, or that you were about to be fined for some transgression or for damage to the client's property. But I knew that the Professor's limited memory made a complaint from him unlikely, and I had kept my promise to his sister-in-law to avoid bothering her; so, I reassured myself that the Director probably just wanted to know how I was managing with a client who had nine blue stars from previous housekeepers.

"I'm afraid this is serious," he said almost before I'd taken my seat, bursting my little bubble of self-delusion. "There's been a complaint." He was rubbing his high forehead and looking terribly pained.

"What sort of complaint?" I stammered.

I had been the subject of complaints before, but in each case the Director had seen immediately that it was the result of a misunderstanding or some eccentricity on the part of the client, and he had simply told me to make the best of the situation. But this time was different.

"Don't play dumb with me," he said. "You spent the night at your client's house?"

"I've done nothing wrong. Who made such a ridiculous, disgusting suggestion?"

"It's not a 'suggestion.' You stayed there, didn't you?"

I nodded meekly.

"You know perfectly well that you must let the agency know if you plan to work overtime, and in the case of an emergency, you have to get the client's written approval for overtime pay."

"Yes, I know," I said.

"Then you broke the rules, and the accusation is not 'ridiculous.'"

"But it wasn't overtime. I was just taking care of my client . . . though I might have gone a little overboard."

"If it wasn't overtime, what was it? If you weren't working when you stayed the night at a male client's house, I think you'll agree it sounds a little suspicious."

"But he was ill! He had a fever and I couldn't leave him alone. I was wrong to ignore the rules, and I'm sorry. But I was only doing what any good housekeeper would do."

"And what about your son?" The Director changed tack, tracing the edge of the Professor's client card with his finger. "I made a special exception for you. I'd never allowed anyone to take a child along to work, but since it seemed as though it was the client's wish, and it was an unusually difficult situation, I decided to let it go. But I immediately started getting complaints from the other girls that I was playing favorites, so I needed you to be beyond reproach on this job."

"I'm sorry, really I am. I was careless. And I'm grateful for your help with my son. . . ."

"I'm taking you off the job," he said. I started to object but he went on. "You're done there. Take today off, and then tomorrow you'll go for an interview at a new place." He turned over the Professor's card and added a tenth blue star.

"Wait a minute. This is all too quick. Who wants me fired? Is it the Professor?"

"It's the client's sister-in-law."

"But I haven't seen her since the interview," I said, shaking my head. "And I don't remember having done anything to offend her. She made me promise not to bother her with the Professor's problems, and I haven't. I realize she pays my salary, but she doesn't know a thing about what goes on in the Professor's house. How can she fire me?"

"She knows you stayed overnight with him."

"She was spying on us?"

"She has every right to keep an eye on you while you're at work."

I remembered having seen someone by the gate in the hedge that night.

"The Professor is sick, and he needs special care. If I don't go to him today, he'll be in a bad way. He's probably getting up right now, all alone, reading his notes. . . ."

"There are plenty of other housekeepers who can look after him," said the Director, cutting me off. He opened the drawer in his desk and filed away the card. "This is not negotiable," he said. "We're done here."

And that was how I came to leave my job at the Professor's house.

My new employers were a couple who ran a tax consulting service. It took more than an hour by train and bus to reach their home, and my duties often lasted until nine o'clock at night. They tended to blur the line between tasks I would normally do in the house and things they asked me to do for their business, and the woman had a cruel streak. But worst of all, Root was once more a latchkey kid. It was the Director's way of punishing me.

In my line of work, you get used to saying good-bye to employers, and all the more so when you work for an agency like the Ake-bono. The clients' needs change constantly, and you almost never find a truly ideal fit between housekeeper and household. What's more, the longer you stay in the same job, the greater the potential for conflict.

A few of my previous employers had been kind enough to give me a going-away party when I left, and I'd been quite tearful once or twice when a child had brought me a good-bye present. But just as frequently a job would end without so much as a parting word, and sometimes I would even receive a bill for damage I had allegedly done to dishes, furniture, or clothing.

However a job ends, I had always tried to take it in my stride. There was nothing personal about it, no cause to feel sad or wounded. To them, I was just one more housekeeper in a long line, not someone to be remembered after I was gone. I usually forgot them, too, as soon as I was out the door. And by the next day, I was too busy learning the rules and expectations for my new job to have time to feel sentimental.

With the Professor, however, things were different. And to be honest, what bothered me most was knowing that he would have no memory that we had ever been there. He could never ask his sister-in-law why I had quit or what had become of Root; and he would never remember us as he sat watching the evening star from his easy chair, or when he paused in the middle of a math problem. It was painful to think about. I was sad, but also angry with myself for having broken something that could never be fixed.

My new job was mindless but physically demanding (washing five fancy imported cars, mopping all the staircases in a four-story building, making dinner for ten), but I still found it difficult to concentrate, since one corner of my brain was always occupied with thoughts of the Professor. And I invariably pictured him as I'd seen him during his illness, sitting on the edge of the bed, bent almost double. Preoccupied as I was with this thought, I made a number of minor mistakes at work, and I was constantly in trouble with the lady of the house.

I didn't know who had taken my place at the Professor's. I hoped it was someone who looked enough like me to match the portrait on the Professor's suit. Was he asking her telephone number or shoe size and then expounding on the mysteries hidden in them? I have to admit that I didn't like to imagine him sharing his secrets with my successor. When I thought about it, the pleasures of our shared mathematical discoveries seemed to fade—though I knew from the Professor that the numbers themselves went on just as they always had, regardless of changes in the world.

Sometimes I imagined that the new housekeeper would be completely overwhelmed by the challenge of working for the Professor, and that the Director would realize I was the only one for the job. But I forced myself to give up such daydreams. It was vain to assume that he couldn't get along without me; the Director had been right, there were plenty of other housekeepers for the job.

Root would often ask why we weren't going to the Professor's anymore.

"The situation changed," I told him.

"What situation?"

"It's complicated." He shrugged, but I could sense his disapproval.

A week after I left the Professor's, the Tigers' Yufune pitched a no-hitter against the Hiroshima Carp. Root and I skipped our baths and listened to the game on the radio after dinner. Mayumi had three RBIs and Shinjo hit a homer. It was 6-0 in the bottom of the eighth—same score as the Nakagomi game. When the Carp went down in order, the noise in the ballpark and the announcer's tone seemed to ratchet up a notch, but Root and I grew quiet. The first Hiroshima batter in the ninth grounded out to second. Root sighed. Each of us knew what the other was thinking, the memories that this stirred up. No need to say anything.

Then Shoda, the last batter, made contact, he popped it up into the outfield, the roar of the crowd drowned out the announcer, and when he finally broke through again, he was still yelling "Out! Out! Out!" over and over again.

"He did it." Root's tone was subdued. I nodded.

"This is the fifty-eighth no-hitter . . . in major league history." The announcer was coming through fitfully. "And the first for the Tigers . . . in nineteen years, since Enatsu in 1973."

We weren't sure whether we were happy or not about Yufune's achievement. The Tigers had won, and it was a great feat to pitch a no-hitter. But somehow the achievement had left us depressed. The excitement pouring from the radio had brought back the game on June 2, and along with it the realization that the Professor, who had sat so happily in seat 714, was far away from us now. And I couldn't help feeling that the foul ball off the bat of that nameless pinch hitter in the ninth, the ball that had nearly hit Root, had been an ill omen.

"Okay, time for bed. You have school in the morning," I said. Root grunted and turned off the radio.

The foul ball foretold the end of Nakagomi's no-hitter. But more bad luck had followed close behind with the Professor's fever and then my dismissal. Of course, there was no way to know if it was all due to the curse of the foul, but to me it certainly felt that way—at that moment, everything had turned for the worse.

One day, at the bus stop on my way to work, a strange woman tricked me out of some money. She wasn't a pickpocket or a purse-snatcher. I willingly gave her the money, so I couldn't go to the police; if she was practicing some new sort of swindle, then it certainly was an effective one. She marched straight up to me, held out her hand, and without any preamble said just one word: "Money." She was a large, pale woman in her late thirties, and other than the fact that she was wearing a spring coat in summer, there was nothing odd about her appearance. She was too neatly dressed to be a vagrant, nor did she seem to be deranged. Her manner was as calm as if she were simply asking directions—in fact she behaved as though I had asked for directions *from her.*

"Money," she said again.

I took out a bill and laid it on her palm. I have no idea why I did it. Why would someone as poor as I am give money to a stranger, short of being threatened at gunpoint? But I did, and having slipped the bill into her pocket, she walked off as grandly as she'd come, just as the bus pulled up to the stop.

All the way to the tax consultants' house, I tried to imagine what my money would mean to this woman. Would it feed her hungry children? Or buy medicine for her ailing parents? Or was it just enough to keep her from going crazy, committing suicide and taking her whole family with her? But no matter how much I tried to convince myself that she really needed it, I couldn't get over my anger at what had happened. It wasn't the loss of the money that upset me; it was the miserable feeling that somehow I was the one who had received some sort of handout, not the other way around.

A few days later, Root and I went to tend my mother's grave on the anniversary of her death. In the thicket behind the gravestone, we discovered a dead fawn. The body was quite decayed, but strips of spotted fur clung to its back. Its legs were splayed out under it, as if it had struggled to stand up right to the end. The organs had liquefied, the eyes were black holes, its jaw was slightly parted, revealing little teeth.

Root found it. He gave a stifled cry, but then stood there frozen, no more able to open his mouth and call me than to look away.

It had probably come running down the mountain and crashed into the stone, dying on the spot. When we looked closer, we could see traces of blood and skin on the grave.

"What should we do?" Root asked.

"It's okay," I told him. "We should just leave it."

We prayed longer that day for the fawn than we did for my mother's soul. We prayed that the tiny life could go with her on her journey.

The next day, I found a picture of Root's father in the local paper. It seemed he had won a research prize given by some foundation. It was just a short article with a blurry picture of a man ten years older than when I had known him, but there was no doubt it was him.

I closed the paper, crumpled it into a ball, and threw it in the garbage. Then, thinking better of it, I fished it out, smoothed the wrinkles, and cut out the article. It looked like a little piece of trash.

"What's the big deal?" I asked myself. "No big deal at all," I replied. "Root's father won a prize. Happy day. That's it."

I folded the article and put it away in the box that held the stump of Root's umbilical cord.

7

I thought of the Professor whenever I saw a prime number—
which, as it turned out, was almost everywhere I looked: price tags
at the supermarket, house numbers above doors, on bus sched-
ules or the expiration date on a package of ham, Root's score on a
test. On the face of it, these numbers faithfully played their official
roles, but in secret they were primes and I knew that was what
gave them their true meaning.

Of course, I couldn't always tell immediately whether a number
was prime. Thanks to the Professor, I knew the prime numbers up
to 100 just by their feel; but when I encountered a larger number

that I suspected might be prime, I had to divide it to be sure. There were plenty of cases where a number that looked to be composite turned out to be prime, and just as many others where I discovered divisors for a number that I was certain was prime.

Taking my cue from the Professor, I started carrying a pencil and a notepad around in the pocket of my apron. That way, I could do my calculations whenever the mood struck. One day while I was cleaning in the kitchen in the tax consultants' house, I found a serial number engraved on the back of the refrigerator door: 2311. It looked intriguing, so I took out my notepad, moved aside the detergent and the rags, and set to work. I tried 3, then 7, and then 11. All to no avail. They all left a remainder of 1. Next I tried 13, and 17, and 19, but none of them was a divisor. There was no way to break up 2,311; but, more than that, its indivisibility was positively devious. Every time I thought I had spotted a divisor, the number seemed to slip away, leaving me oddly exhausted yet all the more eager for the hunt—which was always the way with primes.

Once I'd proved that 2,311 was prime, I put the notepad back in my pocket and went back to my cleaning, though now with a new affection for this refrigerator, which had a prime serial number. It suddenly seemed so noble, divisible by only one and itself.

I encountered 341 while I was scrubbing the floor in their office. A blue tax document, Form 341, had fallen under the desk.

My mop stopped in midstroke. It had to be prime. The form was covered with dust from sitting under the desk for so long, but 341 called out to me; it had all the qualities that would have made it a favorite of the Professor.

My employers had gone home and so I set about checking the number in the darkened office. I hadn't really developed a system for finding divisors, and I ended up relying mostly on intuition. The Professor had shown me a method invented by someone named Eratosthenes, who had been the librarian at Alexandria in ancient Egypt, but it was complicated and I'd forgotten how to do it. Since the Professor had such great respect for intuition when it came to numbers, I suspected he would have been tolerant of my method.

In the end, 341 was not a prime: $341 \div 11 = 31$. A wonderful equation, nonetheless.

Of course, it felt good when a number turned out to be prime. But I wasn't disappointed if it did not. Even when my suspicions proved unfounded, there were still things to be learned. The fact that multiplying two primes such as 11 and 31 yielded a pseudo-prime such as 341, led me in an unexpected direction: I now found myself wondering whether there might be a systematic way to find these pseudo-primes, which so closely resembled true prime numbers.

But despite my curiosity, I set the form on the desk and rinsed my mop in the murky bucket. Nothing would have changed if I'd found a prime number, nor if I'd proven that one wasn't prime. I was still facing a mountain of work. The refrigerator went on keeping things cold, regardless of its serial number, and the person who had filled out Form 341 was still struggling with his tax problems. The numbers didn't make things better; perhaps they even made them worse. Perhaps the ice cream was melting in that refrigerator, I certainly wasn't making any progress mopping the floor, and I suspected my employers would be unhappy with my work. But for all that, there was no denying that 2,311 was prime, and 341 was not.

I remembered something the Professor had said: "The mathematical order is beautiful precisely *because* it has no effect on the real world. Life isn't going to be easier, nor is anyone going to make a fortune, just because they know something about prime numbers. Of course, lots of mathematical discoveries have practical applications, no matter how esoteric they may seem. Research on ellipses made it possible to determine the orbits of the planets, and Einstein used non-Euclidean geometry to describe the form of the universe. Even prime numbers were used during the war to create codes—to cite a regrettable example. But those things aren't the goal of mathematics. The only goal is to discover the truth." The Professor always said the word *truth* in the same tone as the word *mathematics*.

"Try making a straight line right here," he'd said to me one evening at the dinner table. Using a chopstick for a ruler, I traced a line on the back of an advertising leaflet—our usual source of scrap paper. "That's right. You know the definition of a straight line. But think about it for a minute: the line you drew has a beginning and an end. So it's actually a line 'segment'—the shortest distance connecting two points. A true line has no ends; it extends infinitely in either direction. But of course, a sheet of paper has limits, as do your time and energy, so we use this segment provisionally to represent the real thing. Now furthermore, no matter how carefully you sharpen your pencil, the lead will always have a thickness, so the line you draw with it will have a certain width, it will have a surface area, and that means it will have *two* dimensions. A real line has only *one* dimension, and that means it is impossible to draw it on a piece of real paper."

I studied the point of the pencil.

"So you might wonder where you would ever find a real line— and the answer would be, only in here." Again, he pointed at his chest, just as he had when he had taught us about imaginary numbers. "Eternal truths are ultimately invisible, and you won't find them in material things or natural phenomena, or even in human emotions. Mathematics, however, can illuminate them, can give them expression—in fact, nothing can prevent it from doing so."

As I mopped the office floor, my mind churning with worries about Root, I realized how much I needed this eternal truth that the Professor had described. I needed the sense that this invisible world was somehow propping up the visible one, that this one, true line extended infinitely, without width or area, confidently piercing through the shadows. Somehow, this line would help me find peace.

I had just got back from shopping and was about to start dinner for the tax consultants when a call came from the secretary at the Akebono Housekeeping Agency.

"Get right over to that mathematician's house. It seems your son has done something to upset them. I don't know what happened, but get over there now. That's an order from the Director."

She hung up before I'd had time to find out more.

I remembered immediately the curse of the foul ball. At first, I'd mistaken it for good luck when the ball missed Root, but it seemed to have come back to haunt us, to fall right on his head. The Professor had been right: "You should never leave a child alone."

Maybe he had choked on the donut I'd given him as a snack. Or he'd gotten a shock trying to plug in the radio. Frightening images ran through my head. I didn't know what to tell my employer as I ran off to the Professor's, her glare following me out the door.

It had been less than a month since we'd left the cottage. The broken doorbell, the dilapidated furniture, and the overgrown garden were the same, but the minute I stepped inside I had a bad feeling.

It was clear that Root had not been hurt, which came as a relief. He hadn't suffocated or been electrocuted but was sitting next to the Professor at the table, his school backpack at his feet.

The bad feeling was coming from the Professor's sister-in-law, who was sitting across from them. Next to her was a middle-aged woman I had never seen before—my replacement, I assumed. There was something indescribably unpleasant about seeing these intruders in a space occupied, in my memory, by just the three of us, the Professor, Root, and me.

As my feeling of relief faded, I began to realize how odd it was for Root to be here. The widow sat at the table, in the same sort of elegant dress she had worn during my interview. She held her cane firmly in her left hand. Root seemed completely cowed and refused to even look up at me. The Professor had assumed his "thinking" pose, staring intently off into the distance, acknowledging no one.

"I'm sorry to call you away from work," said the widow. "Please, have a seat." She pointed to a chair. I was so out of breath after running from the station that I forgot to give a proper answer. "Please, sit down," she said again. "And you, get our guest some tea, please." The other woman—I had no idea whether or not she was an Akebono employee—got up and went to the stove. The widow's tone was polite, but I could see that she was upset by the way her tongue darted over her lips, and the way her fingers drummed on the table. Unable to think of something to say, I did as I was told and sat down. We were silent for a moment.

"You people . . . ," she began at last, tapping a fingernail on the table again. "What is it you want?" I took a breath before answering.

"Has my son done something wrong?"

Root was staring down at his lap, where he held his Tigers cap, nervously crumpling it in his hands.

"I'll ask the questions, if you don't mind. The first thing I'd like to know is why your boy needs to come to my brother-in-law's house." The polish on her perfect nails was flaking off as she tapped on the table.

"I didn't mean to—" Root started, still not looking up.

"The child of a housekeeper who has left our employ," the widow interrupted him. Though she had said "child" more than once, she made no attempt to look at Root—or at the Professor— as though neither of them was in the room.

"I don't think it's a question of 'need,' " I said, still unsure what she was getting at. "I think he just wanted to pay the Professor a visit."

"I borrowed *The Lou Gehrig Story* from the library, and I wanted to read it with him," Root said, looking up at last.

"Why would a ten-year-old child pay a visit to a sixty-year-old man?" She ignored Root's explanation.

"I'm sorry my son came here without my permission, and I am very sorry if he bothered you. I apologize for failing to supervise him properly."

"That's not the point. I want to know why a housekeeper who has been let go would send her son to see my brother-in-law. What is it you want from him?"

"Want? I'm afraid there's some misunderstanding. He's just a little boy who wanted to visit a friend. He found an interesting book and he wanted to read it with the Professor. Isn't that enough of a reason?"

"I'm sure it is. I'm not implying that the boy had any ulterior motive. I'm asking what you wanted in sending him here."

"I don't want anything, except for my son to be happy."

"Then why do you involve my brother-in-law? You took him out at night, you stayed later than was called for. I don't remember asking you to do any of that."

The housekeeper brought over the tea. She set it in front of us without a word or so much as a clink of the cups and went straight back to the bedroom. It was obvious she would not be taking my side on this.

"I realize that I was out of line, but I can assure you I had no ulterior motive. It was all very innocent."

"Is it about money?"

"Money?!" The word was so unexpected that I nearly shouted it back at her. "How can you say such a thing?"

"I can think of no other reason why you'd indulge my brother-in-law like this."

"Don't be ridiculous!"

"You were fired. You have no business being here!"

"Excuse me," the new housekeeper interrupted, standing in the kitchen doorway. She had removed her apron and was holding her purse. "I'll be going now." She left as quietly as she'd come. We watched as she slipped out the door.

The Professor seemed lost in thought; Root's cap was crushed almost beyond recognition. I took a deep breath.

"It's because we're friends," I said. "Is it a crime to visit a friend?"

"And who is friends with whom exactly?"

"My son and I, with the Professor."

"I'm afraid you've been deceiving yourself," the widow said, shaking her head. "My brother-in-law has no property. He squandered everything on his studies, and he has nothing to show for it."

"And what does that have to do with me?"

"He has no friends, you understand? No one has ever come to visit him."

"Then Root and I are his *first* friends," I said.

At that moment, the Professor stood up.

"Leave the boy alone!"

He took a scrap of paper from his pocket and jotted something down. Setting it on the table, he walked out of the room. His manner had been utterly resolute, as if he'd decided from the beginning that this was the only course of action. There had been no anger or hesitation, he was calmly determined.

We stared at the note. No one moved. On the paper he had written a single line, one simple formula:

$$e^{\pi i} + 1 \quad 0$$

No one spoke. The widow's fingernails had ceased their tapping. Her eyes, so full of suspicion and disdain a moment earlier, now looked at me with a calm, understanding gaze, and I could tell then that she knew the beauty of math.

Not long after that, I received a message from the agency asking me to report for work again at the Professor's house. I could not say whether the widow had a change of heart, or had simply never liked the new housekeeper. I also had no way of determining whether the absurd misunderstanding had been settled or not. But the Professor had now earned his eleventh star.

No matter how many times I went over the strange scene in my mind, it remained a mystery. Why did the widow report me to the agency and have me fired? Why had she reacted so strongly to Root's visit? I was sure she had spied on us from the garden that night after the baseball game, and when I imagined her dragging her bad leg behind her and hiding in the bushes, I almost forgot my anger and felt sorry for her.

The mention of money was probably nothing more than a smoke screen. Maybe the widow was jealous. In her own way, she had been lavishing affection on the Professor for years, and to her I was an interloper. Forbidding me to communicate with the main house was her way of preventing me from disturbing their relationship.

I started work again on July 7, the day known as Tanabata, the Star Festival. The notes fluttering on the Professor's jacket as he met me at the door reminded me of the strips of colored paper on which children write their wishes for the festival. My portrait and the square root sign next to it were still clipped to his cuff.

"How much did you weigh at birth?" This question was new to me.

"I was 3,217 grams," I said. Having no idea what my own weight had been, I used Root's.

"Two to the 3,217th minus 1 is a Mersenne prime," he mumbled before disappearing into his study.

During the previous month, the Tigers had managed to climb back into the pennant race. After Yufune's no-hitter, the strength of the pitching staff had given a boost to the offense as well. But at the end of June things started to unravel. They had lost six straight, and the Giants had managed to pass them, bumping the Tigers down to third place.

The housekeeper who had pinch-hit for me had been methodical, and while I had been afraid to disturb the Professor's work and had barely touched the books in his study, she had picked them all up and stuffed them into the bookshelves, stacking any that didn't fit in the spaces above the armoire and under the sofa. Apparently she had a single organizing principle: size. In the wake of her efforts, there was no denying that the room looked neater, but the hidden order behind the years of chaos had been completely destroyed.

I suddenly remembered the cookie tin filled with baseball cards and went to look for it, fearing it had been lost. It was not far from where I'd left it, now being used as a bookend. The cards inside were safe and sound.

But whether the Tigers rose or fell in the rankings, whether or not his study was neat, the Professor remained the same. Within two days, the interim housekeeper's efforts had vanished and the study had returned to its familiar state of disarray.

I still had the note the Professor had written the day of my confrontation with his sister-in-law. She hadn't seen me take it; I'd slipped it safely away into my wallet next to a photograph of Root.

I went to the library to find out about the formula. The Professor would certainly have explained it to me if I'd asked, but I felt that I would have a much deeper understanding if I struggled with it alone for a while. This was only a feeling, but I realized that during my short acquaintance with the Professor I had begun to approach numbers in the same intuitive way I'd learned music or reading. And my feelings told me that this short formula was not to be taken lightly.

The last time I'd been to the library was to borrow books on di-
nosaurs for a project Root had been assigned during his school vacation last summer. The mathematics section, at the very back of
the second floor, was silent and empty.

In contrast to the Professor's books, which showed signs of
their frequent use—musty jackets, creased pages, crumbs in the
binding—the library books were so neat and clean, they were almost off-putting. I could tell that some of them would sit here forever without anyone cracking their spines.

I took the Professor's note from my wallet.

$$e^{\pi i} + 1 \quad 0$$

His handwriting was unmistakable: the rounded forms, the wa-
vering lines. There was nothing crude or hurried about it; you
could sense the care he had taken with the signs and the neatly
closed circle of the zero. Written in tiny symbols, the formula appeared almost modest, sitting alone in the middle of the page.

As I studied it more closely, the Professor's formula struck me
as rather strange. Although I could only compare it to a few similar formulas—the area of a rectangle is equal to its length times its
width, or the square of the hypotenuse of a right triangle is equal
to the sum of the squares of the other two sides—this one seemed
oddly unbalanced. There were only two numbers—1 and 0—and
one operation—addition. While the equation itself was clear
enough, the first element seemed too elaborate.

I had no idea where to begin researching this apparently simple
equation. I picked up the nearest books and began leafing through
them at random. All I knew for sure was that they were math
books. As I looked at them, their contents seemed beyond the

comprehension of human beings. The pages and pages of complex, impenetrable calculations might have contained the secrets of the universe, copied out of God's notebook.

In my imagination, I saw the creator of the universe sitting in some distant corner of the sky, weaving a pattern of delicate lace so fine that even the faintest light would shine through it. The lace stretches out infinitely in every direction, billowing gently in the cosmic breeze. You want desperately to touch it, hold it up to the light, rub it against your cheek. And all we ask is to be able to re-create the pattern, weave it again with numbers, somehow, in our own language; to make even the tiniest fragment our own, to bring it back to earth.

I came across a book about Fermat's Last Theorem. As it was a history of the problem, not a mathematical study, I found it easier to follow. I already knew that the theorem had remained unsolved for centuries, but I had never seen it written down:

"For all natural numbers greater than 3, there exist no integers x, y, and z, such that: $x^n + y^n = z^n$.

Was this all there was to it? At first glance it seemed that any number of solutions could be found. If $n = 2$, you get the wonderful Pythagorean theorem; did that mean that by simply adding 1 to *n,* the order was irrevocably lost? As I flipped through the book, I learned that the proposition had never been published in a formal thesis but was something Fermat had scribbled in the margins of another document; apparently he had not left a proof, having run out of space on the page. Since then, many geniuses have tried their hand at solving this most perfect of mathematical puzzles, all to no avail. It seemed sad that one man's whim had been bedeviling mathematicians for more than three centuries.

I was impressed by the delicate weaving of the numbers. No

matter how carefully you unraveled a thread, a single moment of inattention could leave you stranded, with no clue what to do next. In all his years of study, the Professor had managed to glimpse several pieces of the lace. I could only hope that some part of him remembered the exquisite pattern.

The third chapter explained that Fermat's Last Theorem was not simply a puzzle designed to excite the curiosity of math fanatics, it had also profoundly affected the very foundations of number theory. And it was here that I found a mention of the Professor's formula. Just as I was aimlessly flipping through pages, a single line flashed in front of me. I held the note up to the page and carefully compared the two. There was no mistake: the equation was Euler's formula.

So now I knew what it was called, but there remained the much more difficult task of trying to understand what it meant. I stood between the bookshelves and I read the same pages several times. When I was confused or flustered, I did as the Professor had suggested and read the lines out loud. Fortunately, I was still the only person in the mathematics section, so no one could complain.

I knew what was meant by π. It was a mathematical constant—the ratio of a circle's circumference to its diameter. The Professor had also taught me the meaning of i. It stood for the imaginary number that results from taking the square root of -1. The problem was e. I gathered that, like π, it was a nonrepeating irrational number and one of the most important constants in mathematics.

Logarithm was another term that seemed to be important. I learned that the logarithm of a given number is the power by which you need to raise a fixed number, called the base, in order to produce the given number. So, for example, if the fixed number, or base, is 10, the logarithm of 100 is 2: $100 = 10^2$ or $\log_{10}100$.

The decimal system uses measurements whose units are powers of ten. Ten is actually known as the "common logarithm." But logarithms in base e also play an extremely important role, I discovered. These are known as "natural logarithms." At what power of e do you get a given number?—that was what you called an "index." In other words, e is the "base of the natural logarithm." According to Euler's calculations: $e = 2.71828182845904523536028. \ldots$ and so on forever. The calculation itself, compared to the difficulty of the explanation, was quite simple:

$$e = 1 + \frac{1}{1} + \frac{1}{1 \times 2} + \frac{1}{1 \times 2 \times 3} + \frac{1}{1 \times 2 \times 3 \times 4} + \frac{1}{1 \times 2 \times 3 \times 4 \times 5} + \cdots$$

But the simplicity of the calculation only reinforces the enigma of e.

To begin with, what was "natural" about this "natural logarithm"? Wasn't it utterly unnatural to take such a number as your base—a number that could only be expressed by a sign: this tiny e seemed to extend to infinity, falling off even the largest sheet of paper. I could not begin to understand this never-ending number. It seemed as chaotic and random as a line of marching ants or a baby's alphabet blocks, and yet it obeyed its own inner sort of logic. Perhaps there was no fathoming God's notebooks after all. In the entire universe there were only a handful of especially gifted human beings able to understand a tiny part of this order, and then there were the rest of us, who could barely appreciate their discoveries.

The book was so heavy I needed to rest my arms for a moment before flipping back through the pages. I wondered about Leonhard Euler, who was probably the greatest mathematician of the eighteenth century. All I knew about him was this formula, but reading it made me feel as though I were standing in his presence. Using a profoundly unnatural concept, he had discovered the natural connection between numbers that seemed completely unrelated.

If you added 1 to e elevated to the power of π times i, you got 0: $e^{\pi i} + 1 = 0$.

I looked at the Professor's note again. A number that cycled on forever and another vague figure that never revealed its true nature now traced a short and elegant trajectory to a single point. Though there was no circle in evidence, π had descended from somewhere to join hands with e. There they rested, slumped against each other, and it only remained for a human being to add 1, and the world suddenly changed. Everything resolved into nothing, zero.

Euler's formula shone like a shooting star in the night sky, or like a line of poetry carved on the wall of a dark cave. I slipped the Professor's note into my wallet, strangely moved by the beauty of those few symbols. As I headed down the library stairs, I turned back to look. The mathematics stacks were as silent and empty as ever—apparently no one suspected the riches hidden there.

The next day, I returned to the library to look into something else that had been bothering me for a long time. When I found the bound volume of the local newspaper for the year 1975, I read through it a page at a time. The article I was looking for was in the September 24 edition.

On September 23, at approximately 4:10 P.M., on National Highway . . . a truck belonging to a local transport company crossed the center line, causing a head-on collision with a car . . .

Professor of Mathematics . . . suffered severe head injuries and is in critical condition, while his sister-in-law, who was in the passenger seat, is in serious condition with a broken leg. The driver of the truck suffered only minor injuries and is being interviewed by police, who suspect he fell asleep at the wheel.

I closed the volume, remembering the sound of the widow's cane.

I still have the Professor's note, though the photograph of Root has long since faded. Euler's formula comforts me—it is a memento that I still treasure.

I've often asked myself why the Professor wrote this particular formula at that moment. Simply by writing out this one equation and placing it between us, he put an end to the argument between myself and the widow. And as a result, I returned to work as his housekeeper and the Professor renewed his friendship with Root. Had he been calculating this outcome from the beginning? Or, in his confusion, had he simply written a formula at random? There was no way to tell.

What was certain was the Professor's affection for Root. Fearful that Root would think he had caused the argument, the Professor came to his rescue in the only way he knew how. After all these years, I'm still at a loss for words to describe how purely the Professor loved children—except to say that it was as unchangeable and true as Euler's formula itself.

My son's needs always took precedence with the Professor, who only sought to protect him. Watching over my son was the Professor's greatest joy. And Root appreciated the Professor's attentions.

He never ignored or took these kindnesses for granted, and acknowledged that they should be fully recognized and respected. I could only marvel at Root's maturity. If I was setting out their snack and gave the Professor a larger portion than Root, he would invariably scold me. It was a matter of principle that the biggest piece of fish or steak or watermelon should go to the youngest person at the table. Even when he was at a critical point with a math problem, he still seemed to have unlimited time for Root. He was always delighted when Root asked a question, no matter what the subject; and he seemed convinced that children's questions were much more important than those of an adult. He preferred smart questions to smart answers.

The Professor also showed concern for Root's physical well-being and watched over him with care. He noticed ingrown hairs or boils long before I did; he didn't stare or touch him in order to discover these things, he simply knew and he would tell me discreetly, so as not to worry Root. I can still recall him whispering in my ear as I was working in the kitchen. "Do you think we ought to do something about that boil?" he might murmur, as if the world were coming to an end. "Children have quick metabolisms. It might suddenly swell up and press on his lymph nodes or even block his windpipe." He was especially anxious when it came to Root's health.

"Fine. I'll pop it with a needle," I'd say—casually enough to get him truly angry.

"But what if it gets infected?!"

"I'll disinfect the needle first over the stove," I would say, teasing him. His concern for Root delighted me, although I didn't show it.

"Absolutely not! You can't kill all the germs like that!" He refused to let up until I had agreed to take Root straight to the doctor.

He treated Root exactly as he treated prime numbers. For him, primes were the base on which all other natural numbers relied; and children were the foundation of everything worthwhile in the adult world.

I still take out that note sometimes and study it. On sleepless nights, or lonely evenings, when tears come to my eyes thinking about friends who are no longer here. I bow my head in gratitude for that one line.

8

It was on the day of the Star Festival that the Tigers lost their seventh game in a row, 1-0 against Taiyo.

I'd had no trouble falling back into the rhythm of the job, despite my month away. And because of the Professor's memory problem, he immediately forgot my misunderstanding with his sister-in-law. For him, no trace of the trouble remained.

I transferred the notes to his summer suit, taking care to fasten them in the same positions, and I rewrote those that were torn or faded.

"In an envelope in the desk, second drawer from the bottom."

"*Theory of Functions,* 2nd edition, pp. 315–372 and *Commentary on Hyperbolic Functions,* volume IV, chapter 1, § 17."

"Medicine to take after meals in manila envelope, on the left in the sideboard."

"Spare razor blades next to the mirror above the sink."

"Thank $\sqrt{}$ for the cake."

Some of the notes were out of date—it had been a month since Root had brought the Professor a little steamed bun he had baked in his home economics class—but it seemed wrong to throw them out. I treated them all with equal respect.

As I read through them, I realized how hard it was for the Profossor to simply get through the day, and how carefully he hid the enormous efforts he made. I tried to work as quickly as possible and not to linger over the notes. When they were all reattached, his summer suit was ready.

For a few weeks, the Professor had been working on an extremely difficult problem, one that would pay the largest cash prize in the history of the *Journal of Mathematics* to the reader who solved it. Indifferent to money, the Professor took pleasure in the difficulty of the problem itself. Checks from the journal were left unopened on the hall table, and when I asked him if he wanted me to cash his prize money at the post office, he shrugged. In the end, I asked the agency to forward them to his sister-in-law.

Just by looking at the Professor, I could tell that the new problem was especially hard. The intensity of his thought seemed to be near breaking point. He would vanish into the study as though he were literally retreating into his mind, and I imagined that his body might actually vaporize into pure contemplation and disappear. But then the sound of his pencil scratching across the paper would break the stillness and reassure me—the Professor was still with us and was making some progress with the proof.

I tried to imagine how he could work through a problem like this over such a long period of time—he basically had to start again from the beginning every morning. To compensate for the loss of his thoughts from the day before, he had only an ordinary notebook and the scribbled notes that covered his body like a cocoon. Since the accident, math was his life, so perhaps it was also what led him to sit down at his desk each day and return to the problem in front of him.

I was considering all of this while making dinner when the Professor suddenly appeared. Usually, when he was wrestling with a problem, I hardly saw him. I wasn't sure whether I would be interrupting his thinking if I spoke to him, so I continued seeding the peppers and peeling the onions. He walked over, leaned against the counter, folded his arms, and stood there staring at my hands. I felt awkward with him watching me, so I went to get some eggs out of the refrigerator, and a frying pan.

"Did you need something?" I asked at last, no longer able to stand the silence.

"No, go on," he said. His tone was reassuring. "I like to watch you cook," he added.

I wondered if the problem had proven so difficult his brain had blown a fuse—but I broke the eggs into a bowl and beat them with my chopsticks. I went on stirring after the spices had dissolved and the lumps were gone, only stopping when my hand had grown numb.

"Now what are you going to do?" he asked quietly.

"Well . . . ," I said, "next . . . , uh, I have to fry the pork." The Professor's sudden appearance had disrupted my usual routine.

"You're not going to cook the eggs now?"

"No, it's best to let them sit, so the spices blend in."

We were alone, Root was off playing in the park. The afternoon sun divided the garden into patches of shadow and dappled light. The air was still, and the curtains hung limply by the open window. The Professor was watching me with the intense stare he normally reserved for math. His pupils were so black they looked transparent, and his eyelashes seemed to quiver with each breath. He was gazing at my hands, which were only a few feet away, but he might have been staring off into distant space. I dusted the pork filets in flour and arranged them in the pan.

"Why do you have to move them around like that?"

"Because the temperature at the center of the pan is higher than at the edges. You have to move them every so often to cook them evenly."

"I see. No one gets the best spot all the time—they have to compromise."

He nodded as if I had just revealed a great secret. The aroma of cooking meat drifted up between us.

I sliced some peppers and onions for the salad and made an olive oil dressing. Then I fried the eggs. I had planned to sneak some grated carrot into the dressing, which now proved impossible with the Professor watching me. He said nothing, but he seemed to hold his breath while I cut the lemon peel in the shape of a flower. He leaned in closer as I mixed the vinegar and oil, and I thought I heard him sigh when I set the piping hot omelet on the counter.

"Excuse me," I said at last, unable to control my curiosity. "But I'm wondering what you find so interesting."

"I like to watch you cook," he said again. He unfolded his arms and looked out the window for the spot where the evening star would appear. Then he went back to his study without a sound. The setting sun shone on his back as he walked away.

I looked at the food I had just finished preparing and then at my hands. Sautéed pork garnished with lemon, a salad, and a soft, yellow omelet. I studied the dishes, one by one. They were all perfectly ordinary, but they looked delicious—satisfying food at the end of a long day. I looked at my palms again, filled suddenly with an absurd sense of satisfaction, as though I had just solved Fermat's Last Theorem.

The rainy season came to an end, Root's summer vacation began, and still the Professor struggled with his proof. I was eagerly looking forward to the day he would ask me to mail it to the magazine.

The weather had turned hot. The cottage had neither air-conditioning nor a cross breeze. Root and I tried not to complain, but we were no match for the Professor's stoicism. At noon, on the hottest day, he would sit at his desk with the doors closed, never removing his jacket—as if he were afraid that all the work he'd done on the proof would crumble if he slipped out of his coat. The notes on his suit had wilted, and he was covered in a painful-looking heat rash, but when I came in with a fan, or suggested a cold shower, or more barley tea, he would chase me out in exasperation.

Once his summer vacation started, Root would come with me to the cottage in the morning. Given my recent run-in with the widow, I thought it best not to increase the amount of time he spent with me at work, but the Professor wouldn't hear of it. He was absolutely convinced that a child on vacation had to be where his mother could watch over him. Root, however, much preferred to be at the park playing baseball with his friends or at the pool, so he was almost never with us.

On Friday, July 31, the proof was finished. The Professor didn't seem very excited, nor did he seem especially exhausted. He calmly handed me the pages, and I ran to the post office to be sure to catch the mail before the weekend. I watched as they stamped the envelope and put it in the bin; then, feeling both excited and relieved, I wandered home slowly, shopping along the way. I bought the Professor new underwear, some sweet-smelling soap, ice cream, jelly, and sweet bean paste.

When I reached home, the Professor no longer knew who I was. I checked my watch—it had only been an hour and ten minutes since I'd left. The Professor's eighty-minute timer had never failed before. His head had always been more accurate than any clock. I took off my watch and held it up to my ear.

"How much did you weigh when you were born?" the Professor said.

At the beginning of August, Root went camping for four nights. The trip was only for children over ten, and Root had been looking forward to it for a long time. It would be his first time away from me, but he showed no signs of fear. When I dropped him off at the bus, clusters of mothers and children were saying their good-byes. The mothers were all issuing last-minute instructions and warnings, and I had a few of my own for Root, telling him to wear his jacket and to hang on to his insurance card—but he never gave me a chance to finish. He was the first one on the bus, and he barely waved good-bye as they pulled away.

The first evening, I lingered at the Professor's, reluctant to go home to my empty apartment after I'd finished washing the dinner dishes.

"Would you like some fruit?"

"That would be nice," the Professor replied, turning to look at me from his easy chair. Though the sun would not be setting for some time yet, thick clouds had gathered, and the light in the garden was mottled, as though the world had been wrapped in lavender cellophane. A gentle breeze blew through the kitchen window. I cut up some melon and took it to the Professor. Then I sat down beside him.

"You should have some, too," he said.

"No, thanks. You go ahead."

He crushed the flesh of the melon with the back of his fork and began to eat, spraying juice on the table.

With Root at camp, there was no one to turn on the radio, the house was quiet. There was no sign of life from the widow's house, either. A single cicada cried for a moment and then fell silent.

"Have a little," he said, holding out the last slice.

"No, thanks. You eat it," I said, wiping his mouth with my handkerchief. "It was hot again today."

"Scorching," he said.

"Don't forget to use the medicine for your heat rash. It's in the bathroom."

"I'll try to remember," he said.

"They say it'll be even hotter tomorrow."

"That's how we spend the summer," he said, "complaining about the heat."

The trees suddenly began to tremble and the sky grew dark. The line of hills on the horizon, faintly visible just a moment before, disappeared in the gloom. There was a rumbling in the distance.

"Thunder!" we said together, as the rain began to fall in enormous drops. The pounding on the roof echoed through the room. I stood up to close the windows, but the Professor stopped me.

"Leave them," he said. "It feels good to have them open."

The curtains billowed in the breeze, letting the rain pour in on our bare feet. It was cool and refreshing, just as the Professor had said. The sun had vanished and the only light in the garden was the faint glow from the lamp above the kitchen sink. Small birds flitted among the drooping, tangled branches of the trees, and then the rain obscured everything. The smell of fresh garden soil filled the air as the thunder drew closer.

I was thinking about Root. Would he find the raincoat I'd packed? And should I have made him take an extra pair of sneakers? I hoped he was eating properly, and that he wouldn't go to bed with wet hair and catch a cold.

"Do you suppose it's raining in the mountains?" I said.

"It's too dark to see," said the Professor, squinting off at the horizon. "I suppose I'll need to get my prescription changed soon."

"Is the lightning over the mountains?" I said.

"Why are you so concerned about the mountains?"

"My son's camping there."

"Your son?"

"Yes. He's ten. He likes baseball and he's a bit of a handful. You nicknamed him Root, because his head is flat on top."

"Is that so, you have a son? That's fine," he said. As soon as Root was mentioned, the Professor cheered up, as usual. "It's a grand thing for a child to go camping in the summer. What could be better for him?"

The Professor leaned back and stretched. His breath smelled faintly of melon. A streak of lightning flashed across the sky, and the thunder rumbled louder than ever. The darkness and heavy rain could not obscure the lightning, and even after a burst had faded, it remained etched on my retina.

"I'm sure that one hit the ground," I said. The Professor grunted but did not answer. The rain splashed over the floor. As I rolled up his cuffs so they wouldn't get wet, his legs twitched as though I were tickling him.

"Lightning tends to strike high places, so the mountains are more dangerous than down here," he said. As a mathematician— a scientist—I thought he would have known more than I did about lightning, but I was wrong. "And the evening star was hazy this evening, which usually means the weather is taking a turn for the worse." There was none of the Professor's usual logic in his pronouncements on the weather.

As he spoke, the rain fell hard. The lightning flashed, the thunder rattled the windowpanes.

"I'm worried about Root," I said.

"Someone once wrote that worrying is the hardest thing about being a parent."

"His clothes are probably soaked, and he's there for four more days. He'll be miserable."

"It's just a shower. When the sun comes out tomorrow and it warms up, everything will dry out."

"But what if he gets struck by lightning?"

"The odds are very low," he said.

"But if he does? What if lightning strikes his Tigers cap? It's flat and shaped like the square root sign; it could attract lightning."

"Pointy heads are more dangerous," he said. "They're like lightning rods."

The Professor was usually the one to worry about Root, but this time he was determined to comfort me. A gust of wind twisted the trees, but as the storm raged on, the cottage seemed to settle into silence. There was a light in a window on the second floor of the widow's house.

"I feel empty when Root isn't here," I said.

I hadn't really been speaking to him, but the Professor murmured in reply, "So, you're saying that there's a zero in you?"

"I suppose that's what I mean," I said, nodding weakly.

"The person who discovered zero must have been remarkable, don't you think?"

"Hasn't zero been around forever?"

"How long is forever?"

"I don't know. For as long as people have been around—wasn't there always a zero?"

"So you think that zero was there waiting for us when humans came into being, like the flowers and the stars? You should have more respect for human progress. We *made* the zero, through great pain and struggle."

He sat up in his chair and scratched his head, looking utterly disheveled.

"So who was it? Who discovered zero?"

"An Indian mathematician; we don't know his name. The ancient Greeks thought there was no need to count something that was nothing. And since it was nothing, they held that it was impossible to express it as a figure. So someone had to overcome this reasonable assumption, someone had to figure out how to express nothing as a number. This unknown man from India made nonexistence exist. Extraordinary, don't you think?"

"Yes," I agreed, though I wasn't sure how this Indian mathematician would calm my worries about Root. Still, I had learned from experience that anything the Professor was passionate about was bound to be worthwhile. "So, a great Indian teacher of mathematics discovered the zero written in God's notebook, and, thanks to him, we can now read many more pages in the notebook. Is that it?"

"That's it exactly." He laughed. He took a pencil and notepaper from his pocket, as I'd seen him do a thousand times. The gesture was always refined. "Take a look at this," he said. "It's thanks to zero that we can tell these two numbers apart." Using the arm of the chair to write on, he scribbled down the numbers 38 and 308. Then he drew two thick lines under the zero. "Thirty-eight is made up of three 10s and eight 1s; 308 is three 100s, no 10s, and eight 1s. The tens place is empty, and it's the 0 that tells us that. Do you see?"

"I do."

"So, let's pretend there's a ruler here, a wooden ruler thirty centimeters long. What would be the mark all the way at the left here?"

"That would be zero."

"That's right. So zero would be on the far left. A ruler begins at zero. All you have to do is line up the edge of what you want to measure with the zero, and the ruler does the rest. If you started with 1, it wouldn't work. So it's zero that allows us to use a ruler, too."

The rain continued. A siren wailed somewhere; the thunder drowned it out.

"But the most marvelous thing about zero is not that it's a sign or a measurement, but that it's a real number all by itself. It's the number that's one less than 1, the smallest of the natural numbers. Despite what the Greeks might have thought, zero doesn't disturb the rules of calculation; on the contrary, it brings greater order to them. Try imagining one little bird sitting on a branch, singing in a clear, high voice. He has a pretty little beak and colorful feathers. You stare at him, enchanted; but as soon as you breathe, he flies away, leaving only the bare branch, and a few dried leaves fluttering in the breeze." The Professor pointed out at the dark garden, as if the bird had really just flown away. The shadows seemed deeper and longer in the rain. "Yes, $1 - 1 = 0$. A lovely equation, don't you think?"

He turned toward me. A loud clap of thunder shook the room, and the light in the main house blinked off for a moment. I gripped the sleeve of his jacket.

"Don't worry," he said, reaching over to stroke my hand. "The square root sign is a sturdy one. It shelters all the numbers."

Needless to say, Root came home safe and sound when his camping trip was over. He brought the Professor a little figurine of a sleeping rabbit he had made from twigs and acorns. The Professor set it on his desk, and at its feet he attached a note: "A present from $\sqrt{}$ (the housekeeper's son)."

I asked Root whether the storm on the first day of his trip had caused problems, but he said they hadn't had a drop of rain. In the end, the only damage from the lightning had been done to a gingko tree at a shrine near the Professor's house.

The heat returned, and with it the buzzing of the cicadas. The curtains and the floor were dry by the next day.

Root's attention turned to the Tigers. He had apparently hoped they would be in first place by the time he got back; but things had not gone his way and they had fallen back to fourth after losing to the first-place Swallows.

"Did you cheer for them while I was gone?"

"Of course we did," said the Professor. Root seemed to suspect that his team's problems had been caused by the Professor's negligence.

"But you don't even know how to turn on the radio."

"Your mother showed me."

"Really?"

"Really. She even tuned in the game for me."

"But they don't win if you just sit there and listen."

"I know, and I truly did cheer for them. I talked to the radio the whole time. I prayed Enatsu would strike out the side every inning." The Professor did everything he could to placate Root.

Soon, we were back to our evenings in the kitchen listening to the radio. The receiver, which was perched on top of the dish cupboard, had worked very well since the Professor had it repaired; and the terrible static that occasionally drowned out the game was due to the poor location of the cottage rather than to the radio itself.

We kept the volume low until the game came on, so low you could barely hear it over the everyday sounds—my puttering in the kitchen before dinner, the motorbikes on the street outside, the Professor muttering to himself, or Root's occasional sneeze. Only when we all fell silent could we hear the music, which always seemed to be some nameless old song.

The Professor was reading in his easy chair near the window. Root was fidgeting at the table, working on something in his notebook. The previous title on the notebook—"Cubic forms with whole-number coefficients, No. 11"—had been scratched out and replaced with "Tiger Notes" in Root's handwriting. The Professor had given him a notebook he no longer needed to record data on the team. The first three pages were filled with incomprehensible equations and the later ones with other esoteric bits of information, such as Nakada's ERA or Shinjo's batting average.

I was kneading bread dough in the kitchen. We had decided to have fresh bread, something we hadn't had in a long while; topped with cheese or ham or vegetables, it would be our dinner.

The sun had set, but the air was stifling, as though the leaves on the trees were breathing back the heat they had absorbed from the long, hot day. A warm blast of air blew in through the windows. The flowers on the morning glory Root had brought home from school had closed up for the night, and cicadas were resting on the trunk of the tallest tree in the garden, a grand old paulownia.

The fresh dough was soft and supple. The counter and floor were white with flour, as was my brow where I'd wiped the sweat with my sleeve.

"Professor?" said Root, his pencil poised above the page. Due to the heat, he wore a sleeveless T-shirt and a pair of shorts. He was just back from the pool and his hair was still wet.

"Yes?" said the Professor, looking up. His reading glasses had slipped to the end of his nose.

"What does 'Total Bases' mean?"

"It's the number of bases a player earns from a hit. So you'd score one for a single, two for a double, three for a triple, and . . ."

"Four for a home run."

"Right!" The Professor was delighted by Root's enthusiasm.

"You shouldn't bother the Professor when he's working," I said, dividing the dough into pieces and rounding them into little balls.

"I know," said Root.

The sky was clear, without a wisp of cloud. Sunlight filtered through the brilliant green leaves of the paulownia tree, dappling the ground in the garden. Root counted out the bases on his fingers as I lit the oven. Static crackled through the music on the radio and then faded again.

"But what about—" Root spoke up again.

"What about what?" I interrupted.

"I'm not asking you," he said. "Professor, how do you calculate 'Regulation at Bats'?"

"You multiply the number of games by 3.1, and discard everything after the decimal point."

"So you round down for .4 and up for .5?" Root asked.

"That's right. Let me have a look." He closed his book and went over to where Root was working. The notes on his jacket made a low, rustling sound. He rested one hand on the table and the other on Root's shoulder. Their shadows merged, with Root's legs swinging back and forth under the chair. I put the little loaves in the oven.

Soon, the music on the radio announced the start of the game. Root turned up the volume.

"Got to win today . . . got to win today . . . got to win today." It was his daily incantation.

"Do you suppose Enatsu will be starting?" the Professor said, taking off his glasses.

As we listened, I remembered the pristine pitcher's mound at the center of the infield, neatly rounded into a cool, damp, black mass awaiting the start of the game.

"Pitching today for the Tigers . . ."

Cheers and static drowned out the voice of the announcer. The smell of baking bread filled the room as we pictured the trail left by the pitcher's cleats on his walk out to the mound.

9

One day toward the end of summer vacation, I noticed that the Professor's jaw was badly swollen. It was just as the Tigers were returning from a successful road trip on which they'd managed to go 10 and 6, vaulting into second place just two and a half games behind the division-leading Yakult.

The Professor had apparently been hiding his problem from me and had not said a word about the pain. If he had given himself one-tenth of the attention that he paid to Root, this sort of thing would never have happened; but by the time I noticed, the left side of his face was so swollen that he could barely open his mouth.

Getting him to the dentist proved easier than our trips to the barber or the baseball game. The pain had taken the fight out of him, and his stiff jaw prevented him from making the usual objections. He changed his shirt, put on his shoes, and followed me out the door. I held a parasol to protect him from the sun, and he huddled underneath, as though hiding from the pain.

"You have to wait for me, you know," he mumbled as we sat down in the waiting room. Then, unsure as to whether I'd understood or whether he could trust me, he repeated himself every few minutes while we waited.

"You can't go out for a walk while I'm in there. You have to sit right here and wait for me. Do you understand?"

"Of course. I'm not about to leave you."

I rubbed his back, hoping to ease the pain a little. The other patients stared at the floor, as embarrassed as I was. But I knew from experience what to do in this situation. You simply had to be resolute, like the Pythagorean theorem or Euler's formula, and to keep the Professor happy.

"Really?" said the Professor.

"Of course. Don't worry. I'll be right here waiting for you, no matter how long it takes."

I knew it was impossible to reassure him, but I repeated myself anyway. As the door to the examination room closed behind him, he turned around as if checking that I'd keep my promise.

The treatment took longer than expected. A number of people who had been called in after the Professor had already settled their bills and gone home, and still he had not reappeared. He rarely brushed his teeth and did little to care for his dentures, and I doubted he was a particularly cooperative patient, so the dentist probably had his hands full. I got up from time to time to try to peer through the receptionist's window, but I could only see the back of the Professor's head.

When he finally emerged from the examination room, his mood was even worse than before. He looked exhausted, and his face was bathed in sweat. His mouth, still numb from the anesthesia, was pinched into an annoyed pout, and he sniffled constantly.

"Are you all right? You must be tired," I said. I stood up and held out my hand to him, but he brushed me aside and walked away without a look.

I called after him, but it was as if he hadn't heard me. He shuffled out of the office slippers, pushed on his shoes, and walked out the door. I paid the bill as quickly as I could and chased after him down the street.

He was reaching a busy intersection when I finally caught up with him. He seemed to know the way home, but he had charged out into the street, oblivious to the traffic and the signals. I was surprised to see how quickly he could walk.

"Wait!" I called out to slow him down, but this only succeeded in drawing wary looks from the people nearby. The heat and glare of the summer sun were dizzying.

I was starting to get angry. He had no reason to be so rude to me. It was hardly my fault that it had been so painful; and it would have been far worse had we ignored it. Even Root was braver than this at the dentist. . . . Of course! That was it! I should have brought Root along. The Professor would have felt compelled to behave more like an adult with a child present. To treat me like this, after I'd kept my promise and waited for him the whole time. . . .

I knew it was cruel, but I had half a mind to let him go off on his own. I slowed my pace and he charged ahead, apparently determined to get home as soon as possible, ignoring the oncoming traffic. His hair was wild, and his suit was rumpled. He looked smaller than usual as his tiny, receding figure disappeared in the evening shadows. The notes on his jacket, catching a glint of sunlight, helped to keep him in sight. They blinked like coded messages, signaling the Professor's whereabouts.

Suddenly, my hand tightened around the handle of my parasol and I checked my watch. I calculated the time from the moment the Professor left the waiting room until he returned. Ten minutes, twenty, thirty . . . I ticked off the intervals. Something was wrong.

I ran after him, shuffling to keep my sandals on my feet, my eyes fixed on the bright scraps of paper clipped to his suit as they disappeared around the corner into the shadows of the city.

While the Professor was taking a bath, I tried to straighten up his issues of the *Journal of Mathematics*. He seemed to live for the puzzle problems it published, but he didn't pay much attention to the rest of magazine and left the barely opened copies strewn around his study. I gathered up all the issues and arranged them in chronological order; then I checked the tables of contents and pulled out the ones in which the Professor was mentioned for having won a prize. That still left quite a few issues. The names of prizewinners were printed in bold type and boxed in a fancy border, so they were easy to spot. The Professor's name seemed especially grand to me, printed there in magazine after magazine; and the proofs themselves, though they lost the familiarity they had in the Professor's own handwriting, seemed all the more impressive in print, the force of their incomprehensible arguments all the more powerful, even to me.

The study was hotter than the rest of the house, perhaps because it had been closed up and silent for so long. As I packed away the issues of the journal that did not mention the Professor, I thought about the dentist's office and I calculated the time again. With the Professor, you always had to keep in mind his eighty-minute memory. Still, no matter how many times I added it up, we'd been apart less than an hour.

I told myself that the Professor was only human, and even though he was a brilliant mathematician, there was no reason why the eighty-minute cycle should be entirely reliable. Circumstances change from day to day, and the people who are subject to them change as well. The Professor had been in pain, and strangers were poking around in his mouth; perhaps this had thrown off his inner clock.

The stack of magazines containing the Professor's work was as high as my waist. How precious they were to me, these proofs he had devised, studded like jewels in an otherwise featureless journal. I straightened the pile. Here was the embodiment of the Professor's labors, and the concrete proof that his abilities had not been lost in that terrible accident.

"What are you doing?" He had finished his bath and was back in the study. His lips were still slack from the Novocain, but his jaw was less swollen. He seemed more cheerful, too, as if the pain had eased. I glanced quickly at the clock on the wall; he had been in the bath for less than thirty minutes.

"I'm straightening up the magazines," I said.

"Well, thank you, I appreciate it. But I don't think I really need to keep them. It's a lot to ask, but would you mind throwing them out?"

"I'm afraid I can't do that."

"Why not?"

"Because they're full of your work," I said, "the wonderful things you've accomplished."

He gave me a hesitant look but said nothing. The water dripping from his hair made blotches on his notes.

The cicadas that had been crying all morning suddenly fell silent. The garden baked under the blinding glare of the summer sun. If you looked carefully, you could see a line of thin clouds beyond the mountains at the horizon, clouds that seemed to announce the coming of autumn. They were just at the spot where the evening star would rise.

Not long after Root started school again, a letter arrived from the *Journal of Mathematics*. The Professor's proof, which he had worked on all summer, had won first prize.

The Professor, of course, showed no sign of pleasure. He barely looked at the letter before tossing it on the table without a word or a smile.

"It's the largest prize in the history of the *Janaruobu*," I pointed out. Afraid I would mangle the pronunciation of the long foreign title, I had taken to calling it simply the *Janaruobu*.

The Professor gave a bored sigh.

"Do you know how hard you worked on that proof? You barely ate or slept for weeks. You literally sweated out the answer—and there are salt rings on your suit to prove it." Knowing he had forgotten all this, I wanted at least to remind him of his efforts. "Well, *I* remember how hard you worked," I said. "And how heavy the proof was when you gave it to me to mail, and how proud I was when I got to the window at the post office."

"Is that so?"

No matter what I said, he barely responded.

Perhaps all mathematicians underestimated the importance of their accomplishments. Or perhaps this was just the Professor's nature. Surely there must be ambitious mathematicians who wanted to be known for the advancements they made in their field. But none of that seemed to matter to the Professor. He was completely indifferent to a problem as soon as he had solved it. Once the object of his attention had yielded, showing its true form, the Professor lost interest. He simply walked away in search of the next challenge.

Nor was he like this only with numbers. When he had carried the injured Root to the hospital, or when he had protected him from the foul ball, it had been difficult for him to accept our gratitude—he was not being stubborn or perverse, he simply couldn't understand what he had done to deserve our thanks.

He discounted the value of his own efforts, and seemed to feel that anyone would have done the same.

"We'll have to celebrate," I said.

"I don't think there's anything to celebrate."

"When someone has worked hard and won first prize, his friends want to celebrate with him."

"Why make a fuss? I simply peeked in God's notebook and copied down a bit of what I saw. . . ."

"No, we're going to celebrate. Root and I want to, even if you don't." As usual, I played the Root card. "And now that you mention it, we could combine this with Root's birthday party. He was born on the eleventh. He'll be delighted to share the celebration with you."

"And how old will he be?" My stratagem had worked. He was finally beginning to show some enthusiasm.

"Eleven," I said.

"Eleven." He sat up and blinked, then ran his hand through his hair.

"That's right. Eleven."

"An exquisite number. An especially beautiful prime among primes. And it was Murayama's number. Truly wonderful, don't you think?" What I thought was that everyone has a birthday once a year, and that was far less interesting than a mathematical proof that had won a major prize; but of course I held my tongue and nodded. "Good! Then we should have a party. Children need to celebrate. Nothing makes them happier than some cake, some candles, and a little applause. That's simple enough, isn't it?"

"Yes, of course," I said. I took a marker and drew a big circle around the eleventh on the calendar, big enough to catch the attention of someone as distracted as the Professor. For his part, he made a new note—"Friday, September 11, Root's eleventh birthday party"—and found a spot for it just below his most important note.

"There," he said, nodding in satisfaction as he studied the new addition. "That should do."

Root and I talked it over and decided that we would give the Professor an Enatsu baseball card at the party. So, while he was napping in the kitchen, we crept into the study and I showed Root the cookie tin. He was immediately fascinated and seemed to forget we were keeping a secret from the Professor. Sitting on the floor, he began to examine each card, reverently admiring their every detail.

"Be careful with them," I fussed nervously. "They're important to the Professor." But Root hardly seemed to hear me.

It was the first time he had really had a chance to look at base-

ball cards. He knew that people collected them—his friends had
shown him theirs—but it was as if he had avoided developing an
interest in them. He was not the sort of boy who would ask his
mother for something frivolous.

But once he had seen the Professor's collection, there was no
going back. Another part of the world of baseball had opened up
before him, and it held a very different appeal from that of the real
game. Each card was a talisman of an imaginary game that was
separate from the one he saw played out on the field or heard on
the radio. A photograph capturing a crucial moment, an inspiring
story, and the historical record inscribed on the back—all captured on a rectangular card in a clean plastic case you could hold
in the palm of your hand. Everything about the cards fascinated
Root, and this particular collection was all the more delightful because it belonged to the Professor.

"Look at this Enatsu! You can even see the sweat flying off
him." "And this one of Bacque—look how long his arms are."
"And this one's unbelievable! When you hold it up to the light,
you get a 3-D picture of Enatsu!" He stopped to show me every
new discovery.

"I know," I said at last. "Now put them back." I'd heard a
creak from the easy chair in the next room. The Professor would
be getting up soon. "You can ask him to show them to you some-
time soon. But be sure you put them back in the right order; he's
got a very special system."

Whether from excitement or because the cards were heavier
than he'd thought, Root dropped the tin. There was a loud crash,
but the cards were so tightly packed together that the damage was
minimal—only a few of the second basemen had scattered across
the floor.

We retrieved them quickly, and fortunately there were no bent corners or cracked cases. The only difference was that we'd spoiled the Professor's incredibly precise order.

I was worried that the Professor could wake up at any moment. I knew he would have been happy to show Root his collection had we simply asked, so I wasn't sure why I was sneaking around like this, or why I was hesitant to raise the subject of the cookie tin. For some reason, I had convinced myself that the Professor would not want other people to see the cards.

"This is Shirasaka, so 'shi' should go right after Kamata Minoru."

"How do you read this one?"

"It's written next to the characters in the syllabary—Hondo Yasuji. So it goes back here."

"Do you know who he is?"

"No, but he must have been important to have a card. We can't worry about that now, we've got to hurry."

As we concentrated on putting the cards back in order, I suddenly noticed something: the tin had a second layer underneath the one holding the cards. I was about to file a Motoyashiki Kingo when I realized that the tin was slightly deeper than the height of the card.

"Hang on a second." Stopping Root for a moment, I wiggled my finger into the space where the second basemen had fallen out. There was no doubt about it: the tin had a false bottom.

"What?" said Root, looking puzzled.

"Nothing," I said. "Just hold on a minute." I had Root fetch a ruler from the desk and I very carefully slipped it under the row of cards. "Look, there's something down there. If I hold them up like this, can you pull it out?"

"Yep, I see it. I think I can get it." Root's small hand slipped into the narrow opening, and in a few seconds he extracted the contents of the hidden compartment.

It was a thesis of some sort. It had been typed in English and was bound with a cover page bearing what looked to be a university seal—a hundred-odd-page mathematical proof. The Professor's name was printed in Gothic letters and the work was dated 1957.

"Is it a problem the Professor solved?"

"It seems to be."

"But why would he hide it here?" Root said, sounding thoroughly mystified. I did a quick mental calculation: 1992–1957—the Professor had been twenty-nine. Since the noises from the next room had stopped, I began to flip through the thesis, the Motoyashiki card still in my hand.

This paper had been handled with as much care as the baseball cards. The paper stock and the type were showing signs of age, but there was no trace of dirt or damage from human hands, no folds or wrinkles or spots—mint condition. The high-quality paper was still soft to the touch and the typist had made no mistakes. The binding, too, was perfect, with the pages neatly gathered at the corners. An edict left by a noble king could hardly have been more carefully produced or preserved.

Taking my cue from those who had handled it so gingerly in the past, and remembering Root's recent mishap, I held it with the greatest care. The paper smelled faintly of cookies, but it still looked impressive, in spite of being pressed down at the bottom of a tin for years under rows of baseball cards.

As for the content, the only thing I could decipher on the first page was the title: Chapter 1. But as I flipped through the pages that followed, I came across the name Artin, and remembered the Artin conjecture that the Professor had explained with a stick in the dirt on the way home from the barber—and the formula he had added when I'd brought up the perfect number 28, and how the cherry blossoms had fluttered to the ground.

Just then, a black-and-white photograph fell from the pages. Root picked it up. It showed the Professor seated on a clover-covered riverbank. He was young and handsome, and he looked completely relaxed with his legs stretched out in front of him. He was squinting slightly in the bright sun. His suit was much like the one he still wore, but, needless to say, there were no notes on his jacket and he seemed to radiate intelligence.

A woman was seated next to the Professor. She leaned timidly toward him, the toes of her shoes poking out from under her flared skirt. Their bodies did not touch, but it was clear that they shared a bond. And in spite of the years that had passed since the picture was taken, I had no doubt that the woman was the Professor's sister-in-law.

There was one more thing I could read. At the top of the cover page, a single line in Japanese:

"For N, with my eternal love. Never forget."

An Enatsu card, we soon realized, was not an easy thing to find. The main problem was that the Professor already owned all of the Enatsu cards from his playing days with the Tigers—that is, before 1975. The later cards all mentioned that he'd been traded, and we had no intention of giving the Professor a card with his hero in a Nankai or Hiroshima uniform.

We started our research by combing through a baseball card magazine (the mere existence of which was news to me), and reading about the types of cards out there, the price range, and the places you could find them. We also learned what we could about the history of baseball cards, the culture of the collectors, and how to protect them. Then, over the weekend, we made a tour of all the nearby shops listed in the back of the magazine

The card shops tended to be in aging office blocks, next to pawnshops, private detective agencies, or fortune-tellers. The dingy elevators were enough to depress me but once we got in the shops, Root was in heaven. The world inside the Professor's tin opened up before him.

At first, his head was turned by each new discovery; but once he had calmed down, we focused on looking for a Yutaka Enatsu card. This section, as we might have guessed, was always among the largest. The shops organized their cards much as the Professor had his cookie tin, with a special place reserved for Enatsu next to other stars such as Sadaharu Oh and Shigeo Nagashima, separated out from the rest of the players who were filed by team or era or position.

I started at the beginning and Root at the end, and we checked every Enatsu card in each shop. It required stamina, like hunting in a dark forest without a compass. But we refused to be discouraged, and we gradually found ourselves perfecting our technique, so that we were able to get through the trays of cards more and more quickly. Lifting a card between thumb and forefinger, we would check the front. If it was obviously one the Professor already owned, we would drop it back. If it was one we hadn't seen, we would check to see whether it met our requirements. We soon found that every card was either already in his collection, or showed Enatsu wearing the wrong uniform. It became clear that the black-and-white cards from the early years that the Professor had collected were extremely rare and quite expensive. Finding a card worthy of his cookie tin was not going to be easy. We flipped through hundreds of Enatsus in several shops. Our fingers would meet in the middle of a bin of cards and we'd realize that we'd come up empty once again.

The shopkeepers never made us feel uncomfortable, even though we spent hours looking without buying anything. When we showed up in search of Enatsu cards, they happily brought out everything they had; and when we were disappointed, they encouraged us to keep looking and not give up hope. At the very last shop on our list, the owner listened to our story and then told us he thought we should try looking for cards that had been used as prizes by a certain candy company back in 1985. The company had always included baseball cards with its candy, but in 1985 it had been celebrating its fiftieth anniversary and had commissioned a run of premium cards. That was the year the Tigers had won the championship, so their players were especially well represented.

"What are 'premium' cards?" Root asked.

"They made all kinds—some had real signatures by the players on them, others had holograms, and some had actual slivers from game bats embedded in them. Since Enatsu was already retired, they did a reissue of the glove card. I used to have one, but it sold right away. They're incredibly popular."

"What's a 'glove card'?" Root wanted to know.

"They cut up a glove and attach scraps of the leather to the card."

"A glove Enatsu actually used?"

"Sure. The Japan Sports Card Federation certified them, so they're genuine. They didn't produce many, and they can be tough to find, but don't give up; there's bound to be one floating around somewhere. If I get one in, I'll give you a call. I have to admit, I'm something of an Enatsu fan myself." He tipped back the brim of Root's Tigers cap and rubbed him on the head—just like the Professor.

The day of the party was approaching. I saw nothing wrong with looking for an alternative present, but Root wouldn't hear of it. He was determined to find a card.

"We can't give up now!" he insisted.

I have no doubt that his primary concern was to make the Professor happy, but it was also true that he had taken a fancy to the whole idea of card collecting, and he had begun to think of himself as a hunter in search of that one elusive card somewhere out there in the great wide world.

The Professor also seemed to be planning for the party in his own way. He had taken to checking the calendar whenever he was in the kitchen. Occasionally, he would go over and trace the circle I'd drawn to mark the eleventh, fingering the note on his chest the whole time. He was remembering the party, but he had no doubt long ago forgotten about the little matter of the *Janaruobu*.

The Professor never found out that we had looked in his cookie tin. I had been momentarily mesmerized by the inscription on the thesis—For N, with my eternal love. Never forget. The handwriting definitely belonged to the Professor, for whom "eternal" meant something more than it did to the rest of us, eternal in the way a mathematical theorem was eternal. . . .

It was Root who brought me back from my daydream.

"Mama, slide the ruler under so I can put it back in." He took the thesis out of my hand and returned it to the bottom of the tin, careful not to disturb or dishonor the Professor's secret.

A moment later, all the cards were back in place, and there was no sign that the collection had ever been touched. The tin itself was undamaged, and the edges of the cards were neatly aligned. Still, something was different. Now that I knew about the thesis and its dedication, the tin was no longer a simple container for baseball cards. It had become a tomb for the Professor's memories. I set it carefully back on the bookshelf.

I hadn't really thought anything would come of the last shopkeeper's suggestion, but somehow I was disappointed when he failed to call. Root made some final efforts, sending off a postcard to the readers' exchange in the magazine and asking around among his friends and their older brothers. Not wanting to be caught without a present, I had quietly arranged a backup. It hadn't been easy to figure out what to buy. I'd thought of pencils and notebooks, clips and note cards, even a new shirt. There were very few things the Professor really needed. The fact that I couldn't discuss the choice with Root made it all the more difficult.

I decided on shoes. He needed a new pair, ones that he could wear anytime, anywhere—mold-free. I bought them and hid them away in the back of the closet, just as I had with Root's presents when he was little. If we did find the card in time, I would slip them into the Professor's shoe cupboard without saying anything.

In the end, a ray of hope came from an unexpected place. I had gone to pick up my paycheck at the Akebono Housekeeping Agency and was talking with some of the other housekeepers. As the Director was listening, I had avoided mentioning the Professor, and just said that my son had been wanting baseball cards and I'd had no luck finding good ones. Then, out of the blue, one of them mentioned that her mother used to run a little store, and she remembered seeing some leftover cards that had been included with candy in a shed where her mother stored old stock.

The first thing that caught my attention was the fact that her mother had retired and closed up the shop in 1985. She had ordered some candy to take on a trip her seniors group was planning, and the chocolates with the cards had been included in the shipment. Thinking the old folks would have no use for them, her mother had peeled off the little black prize envelopes stuck to the back of each box. She'd been planning to give them to a children's club, but had gone into the hospital later in the year and then closed the shop for good. This was how nearly a hundred mint-condition baseball cards had been stored in a shed all this time.

We went straight from the agency to her house, and I headed home with a dusty cardboard box. I told her I wanted to pay her for them, but she flatly refused. In the end, I took them gratefully, not daring to tell her that these discarded prizes were worth far more than the chocolate they had come with.

As soon as I got home, we set to work. I cut the envelopes open while Root removed the cards and checked them. It was a simple process, and we fell into a rhythm. We were now rather experienced with baseball cards, and Root could distinguish between the various types just by touch.

Oshita; Hiramatsu; Nakanishi; Kinugasa; Boomer; Oishi; Kakefu; Harimoto; Nagaike; Horiuchi; Arito; Bass; Akiyama; Kadota; Inao; Kobayashi; Fukumoto. . . . The players appeared one after the other; just as the man at the shop had said, some of the cards had embossed pictures, some had original autographs, and some were actually gilded. Root no longer allowed himself the editorial comments on each card. He seemed to feel that we would achieve our goal more quickly if he concentrated harder. A drift of little black envelopes had begun to collect around me, while the stack of cards Root had collected toppled and scattered between us.

Each time I reached into the box my hand stirred up a moldy odor, mixed with the smell of the chocolate. But by the time we had worked our way through half the box, I had begun to lose hope.

There were too many baseball players. Which was hardly surprising as every team fielded nine players at a time, and there were so many teams that they were divided into Central and Pacific leagues, and the history of the game in Japan spanned more than fifty years. I knew that Enatsu had been a great star, but there were others—Sawamura, Kaneda, Egawa—each of whom had his own fans. So, even with this big stack in front of us, it was unlikely we'd find the one card we wanted. I found myself lowering my expectations, hoping that the effort would at least satisfy Root. After all, I had a perfectly good present hidden in the back of the closet. They weren't particularly fancy shoes, but they were well designed and comfortable-looking, and they had cost considerably more than a baseball card. I was sure the Professor would be pleased with them.

"Ah . . . " Root let out a very grown-up sound, the kind you might make if you'd just discovered the solution to a complex word problem. The little cry was so quiet and restrained that it took me a minute to realize that the card he was holding in his hand was the one we had been looking for. He sat staring at the card, keeping Enatsu to himself for a moment. Neither of us spoke as he showed me the 1985 limited-edition card containing a fragment of Enatsu's own glove.

10

It was a wonderful party, the most memorable one I've ever attended. It was neither elegant nor extravagant—in that sense it had much in common with Root's first birthday party at the home for single mothers, or the Christmases we'd spent with my mother. I'm not sure whether you would even call those other events parties, but I am sure that Root's eleventh birthday was special. It was special because we celebrated it with the Professor, and because it turned out to be the last evening the three of us would ever spend together in the cottage.

We waited for Root to get home from school, and then set

about preparing for the party. I worked on the food while Root mopped the floor in the kitchen and did other little tasks I assigned him. Meanwhile, the Professor ironed the tablecloth.

He had not forgotten his promise. That morning, once he had confirmed that I was the housekeeper and the mother of the child named Root, he had pointed to the circle on the calendar.

"Today is the eleventh," he said, fluttering the note on his chest as if he hoped to be congratulated for having remembered.

I had not intended to ask him to do the ironing. He was so clumsy that it would almost have been safer for Root to do it, and I had been hoping that his only contribution would be to rest as usual in his chair and to stay out of the way. But he had insisted on helping.

"How can I just sit here watching when you've got a little boy working so hard?"

I might have foreseen this objection, but I would never have guessed that he would produce the iron and offer to press the tablecloth. I was astonished that he knew there was an iron in the closet; but when he pulled out the tablecloth, it was like watching a magician performing a sleight of hand. In the six months I'd been working in the cottage, I'd never seen a tablecloth.

"The first thing you need for a party is a clean, ironed cloth on the table," he said. "And I'm quite good with an iron." There was no telling how long the cloth had been stuffed in the back of the closet, but it certainly was a wrinkled mess.

The heat of summer had finally lifted and the air was clear and dry. The shadows in the garden seemed different as well. Although the sky was still light, the moon and the evening star had appeared and the clouds streamed by in ever-changing patterns. Smudges of darkness were beginning to collect around the roots of the trees, but they were still faint, as if the night had agreed to hold off for a bit longer. Evening was our favorite time of the day.

The Professor set up the ironing board on the arms of his easy chair and went to work. From the way he managed the cord to the way he set the temperature, you could tell that he knew what he was doing. He spread out the cloth, and, like the good mathematician he was, divided it into sixteen equal folds.

He sprayed each section with the water bottle, held his hand near the iron to make sure it wasn't too hot, gripped the handle tightly, and pressed down carefully to avoid damaging the fabric. There was a certain rhythm to the way the iron slid across the board. His brow furrowed and his nostrils flared as he forced the wrinkles to submit to his will. He worked with precision and conviction, and even a kind of affection. His ironing seemed highly rational, with a constant speed that allowed him to get the best results with the least effort; all the economy and elegance of his mathematical proofs performed right there on the ironing board.

The Professor was definitely the best man for this job, we had to admit, since the tablecloth was made of delicate lace. All three of us worked together, and we took unexpected pleasure in preparing for the party. The smell of the roast cooking in the oven, the drip-drop of water from the mop, the steam rising from the iron—all blended together and heightened our expectations.

"The Tigers are playing Yakult today," said Root. "If they win, they'll be in first place."

"Do you think they'll win the pennant?" I had just tasted the soup and was checking the oven.

"I'm sure they will," the Professor said, sounding unusually certain. "Look up there," he pointed out the window. "They say it's good luck when there's a little nick out of the bottom edge of the evening star. That means they'll win today and take the pennant."

"What? That isn't true. You're just making it up."

"Up it ingmak just re'you."

No matter how much Root teased him, the Professor's iron kept its rhythm.

Root got down on the floor to clean places that were normally overlooked—the legs of the chairs and the underside of the table. And I went to the dish cupboard in search of a platter for the roast beef. When I looked out again, the garden was deep in shadow.

We were pleased with our work, and looking forward to the food, the presents, and the fun. But at the very last moment, just as we were about to take our places and begin the party, we discovered a little problem. The girl at the bakery had forgotten to put the candles in the box. The cake I'd ordered wasn't large enough to hold eleven candles, so I had asked her to put in one large candle and one small one; but when I pulled the box out of the refrigerator, they were not there.

"We can't have a birthday cake without candles. You don't get your wish if you don't blow them out!" The Professor seemed more upset than the birthday boy himself.

"I'll run back to the bakery and get them," I said, taking off my apron. But Root stopped me before I could get to the door.

"No, I'll go. I'm faster, anyway." And before the words were out of his mouth, he was gone.

The bakery wasn't far away and there was still some daylight left. I closed the cake box and put it back in the refrigerator; then we sat down at the table and waited for Root to return.

The tablecloth looked beautiful. The wrinkles had vanished completely, and its delicate lace pattern had transformed the kitchen. The only decoration was a yogurt bottle with some wild-flowers I had plucked from the garden, but they brightened up the cottage nicely. The knives and forks and spoons didn't match, but they were neatly laid out on the table, and if you scrunched up your eyes the general effect was magnificent.

By comparison, the food was rather plain. I had made shrimp cocktail, roast beef and mashed potatoes, spinach and bacon salad, pea soup, and fruit punch—all Root's favorites—and, for the Professor, no carrots. There were no special sauces or elaborate prepa-rations, it was just simple food. But it did smell good.

I smiled at the Professor and he smiled at me; we were both a bit lost with nothing to do. He coughed, tugged at the collar of his jacket, and squirmed in his chair, anxious for the party to begin.

There was an empty place on the table, just in front of Root's chair—the space I'd saved for the cake. Our eyes fell on it at the same moment.

"Does it seem like he's taking a long time?" the Professor mur-mured, a hint of hesitation in his voice.

"No, I don't think so," I said, surprised to hear him mention the time and see him look at the clock. "It hasn't been ten minutes yet."

"Is that right?"

I turned on the radio to distract him.

"How long has it been now?"

"Twelve minutes."

"Doesn't that seem long?"

"Don't worry. It's fine."

I wondered how many times I had said those words since I'd

come to work at the Professor's house. "Don't worry. It's fine." At the barber, outside the X-ray room at the clinic, on the bus home from the ball game. Sometimes as I was rubbing his back, at other times stroking his hand. But I wondered whether I had ever been able to comfort him. His real pain was somewhere else, and I sensed that I was always missing the spot.

"He'll be back soon. Don't worry." This was all I could offer him.

As it grew darker outside, the Professor's anxiety deepened. Every thirty seconds or so he would pull at his collar and glance at the clock. He was so agitated he didn't seem to notice the notes falling from his chest with each tug.

There were cheers from the radio. Paciorek had a base hit in the bottom of the first and the Tigers had scored.

"How long has it been now?" he asked again. "Something must have happened to him. It's taking too long." The legs of his chair scraped on the floor as he twisted this way and that.

"Okay. I'll go look for him. But you mustn't worry. I'm sure he's fine." I got up and put my hand on his shoulder.

I found Root near the row of shops by the station. The Professor was right, there was a problem. The bakery had been closed. But Root, resourceful as ever, had already come up with a solution. He had found another bakery on the other side of the station, and when he explained the situation they had given him some candles. We turned around and ran straight home to the Professor's.

When we got there, we realized almost immediately that something was wrong. The flowers were as fresh as ever, the Tigers were still leading Yakult, and the food was still laid out for the party, but there had been an accident. In the time it had taken to find two candles, the table had been ruined. The birthday cake lay in a lump in front of Root's place, the very spot where the Professor and I had been staring just a moment ago.

The Professor stood next to the table, still holding the empty cake box. The darkness at his back seemed about to engulf him.

"I thought I'd get it ready. So we could eat it right away," he mumbled without looking up, as if apologizing to the empty box. "I'm so sorry. I don't know what to say. It's ruined. . . ."

We sat him down and did what we could to comfort him. Root took the box from him and tossed it on a chair, as though it hadn't held anything so very important. I turned down the radio and turned on the lights.

"It's not really ruined," I told him. "It'll be fine. Nothing to get upset about."

In a businesslike manner, I set about repairing the damage. The trick was to get everything back to normal as quickly as possible, without giving the Professor time to think.

The cake had fallen from the box, crushing one side. The other half, however, was more or less intact, with most of the chocolate-frosting message still legible: The Professor & Root, Congr— I cut it in three pieces and used a knife to fix the whipped cream. Then I gathered up the scattered strawberries, jelly bunnies, and sugar angels and spread them around as evenly as I could. Finally, I put the candles in Root's piece. "Look!" I announced at last. "Good as new!"

Root peered into the Professor's eyes. "And it'll taste just as good," he said.

"No harm done," I chimed in. But the Professor sat there in silence.

To be honest, I was more worried about the tablecloth than the cake. No matter how much I'd wiped, there were still crumbs and smudges of whipped cream down in the eyelets of the lace. All my scrubbing had only succeeded in filling the room with a sickly sweet smell; but the intricate design of the material had been completely spoiled.

I hid the stain under the platter of roast beef, warmed the soup, and found a match to light the candles. The announcer on the radio said that Yakult had come from behind in the third and was leading the Tigers. Root had the Enatsu card, decorated with a yellow ribbon, hidden in his pocket.

"There, look. Everything's set. Here, Professor, have a seat." As I took him by the hand, he looked up at last and noticed Root standing beside him.

"How old are you?" he murmured. "And what was your name again . . . your head, it's just like the square root sign. . . . We can come to know an infinite range of numbers with this one little sign, even those we can't see. . . ." Then the Professor reached across the table and rubbed Root's head.

11

On June 24, 1993, there was an article in the newspaper about Andrew Wiles, an Englishman teaching at Princeton University. He had proven Fermat's Last Theorem. There were two large pictures stretching across the page, one a photograph of Wiles, a casually dressed man with curly, receding hair, and the other an engraving of Pierre de Fermat, in a flowing seventeenth-century academic gown. In their own funny way, the two pictures told the story of how long it had taken to solve Fermat's riddle. The article praised Wiles's solution as a triumph of the human intellect and a quantum leap in the field. It also noted that Wiles had built on an idea that had been developed by two Japanese mathematicians, Yutaka Taniyama and Goro Shimura, a proposition known as the Taniyama-Shimura conjecture.

When I reached the end of the article, I did what I always did when I thought of the Professor. I took out the scrap of paper folded in my wallet, the one on which he had written Euler's formula: $e^{\pi i} + 1 = 0$.

I was glad to know it was there, this unchanging testament to a peaceful soul.

The Tigers didn't win the pennant in 1992. They might have had a chance if they had won their last two games with Yakult, but they lost 2–5 on October 10 and finished the season in second place, trailing by two games.

Root was distraught at the time, but years later he came to appreciate what a thrill it had been just to have them reach the playoffs. After the 1993 season, they went into a long slump; and still, well into the new millennium, they are perennial cellar-dwellers. Sixth place, sixth place, fifth, sixth, sixth, sixth, sixth. . . . They have changed managers many times; Shinjo went to play in America, Minoru Murayama passed away.

Looking back on it now, the turning point seemed to be that game with Yakult on September 11, 1992. If they had won that game, they might have taken the pennant and perhaps they could have avoided drifting into the slump.

After we'd cleaned up the party at the Professor's and gone home to our apartment, we immediately turned on the radio. The game was in the final innings, tied 3-3. Root soon fell asleep, but I listened to the end.

It was the bottom of the ninth with two outs and a man on first. The count was full when Yagi hit what appeared to be a walk-off home run into the left-field stands. But after the scoreboard had already registered two runs for the Tigers, the third-base umpire waved off the home run, signaling that the ball had hit the post and should be scored as a double. The Tigers protested and the game was stopped for thirty-seven minutes while the umpires deliberated. It was after ten thirty when it resumed, with two out and men on second and third. In the end, the Tigers failed to take advantage of the opportunity and the game went to extra innings with everyone in a sour mood.

As I listened, I thought about the Professor and our parting at the end of the party. Then I took out Euler's formula and studied it again.

I had left the door to Root's room ajar to be able to hear him. From where I sat, I could see the glove that the Professor had given him set carefully next to his pillow. It was a genuine, Little League–certified, leather glove, and he had been thrilled with it. After Root had blown out the candles and we had turned the lights back on, the Professor noticed the notes that had fallen under the table. The timing of the discovery was fortunate, since the first note he saw reminded him where he had hidden Root's gift.

The Professor was not used to giving presents. He held out the package as if he were unsure whether Root would accept it, and when Root came running to hug him and kiss him on the cheek, he squirmed uncomfortably. Root had been reluctant to take off the glove the rest of the evening and would probably have kept it on straight through dinner if I hadn't put my foot down. I found out later from the widow that the Professor had sent her out in search of a "beautiful glove."

At the table that evening, Root and I had done our best to behave as though nothing had happened. After all, the fact that the Professor had forgotten us in less than ten minutes wasn't necessarily cause for concern. We started the party as planned. We had lots of experience dealing with the Professor's memory problems. We would simply adapt to the new situation and cope as best we could.

And yet, something had changed, and, like the cake, I couldn't stop noticing the difference. The more I tried to convince myself there was nothing to worry about, the more troubled I became. But I couldn't let it spoil the party. We laughed and ate to our hearts' content, and talked about prime numbers and Enatsu and the Tigers winning the pennant.

The Professor was delighted to be celebrating an eleven-year-old's birthday. He treated this simple party as though it were an important rite, and I thought of how precious the day of Root's birth was to me, too.

Late that night, as I thought back over our celebration, I traced my finger over Euler's formula, careful not to smudge the soft pencil lines. I could feel with my fingertip the elegant curl of the legs on the π, the certainty and strength of the dot on the i, the decisive way the 0 had been joined at the top.

The game dragged on, and the Tigers missed several chances to end it. I listened through the twelfth, the thirteenth, and the fourteenth innings, unable to shake the nagging feeling that it should have been over a while ago. It was just one run, but they couldn't get it across home plate. The moon rose full and midnight was approaching.

He didn't know much about presents, but the Professor had a genius for receiving them. The expression on his face when Root gave him the Enatsu card was something neither of us will ever forget. He untied the ribbon and looked at the card for a moment. Then he looked up and tried to say something, but his lips just trembled as he held the card to his chest.

The Tigers never did manage to score that run. They stopped the game after fifteen innings, ruling it a tie. They had been at it for six hours and twenty-six minutes.

On Sunday, two days after the party, the Professor moved into a long-term care facility. His sister-in-law called to tell us.

"This is very sudden, isn't it?" I said.

"Actually, we've been planning it for some time. We were just waiting for a bed to open up at the hospital," she said.

"I realize we stayed past working hours the other night. This wouldn't have anything to do with that, would it?"

"No," she said, quite calmly. "I'm not upset about that at all. I knew it would be his last evening with you. But I'm sure you must have noticed what was happening." I wasn't sure what to say. "His eighty-minute tape has broken. His memory no longer goes beyond 1975, not even for a minute."

"I'd be happy to go to the hospital to look after him."

"That won't be necessary. They'll take good care of him. . . . Besides," she said, "I'll be there. You see, my brother-in-law can never remember you, but he can never forget me."

The institution was a forty-minute bus ride from town, behind an abandoned airport. From the windows of the visitor's lounge you could see the cracks in the runway and the weeds growing on the roof of the hangar—and beyond, a thin strip of sea. On clear days, the waves glittered in the sun like a band of light stretched across the horizon.

Root and I went out to see the Professor every month or so. On Sunday mornings we would pack a basket of sandwiches and catch the bus. We would talk awhile in the lounge and then go out on the terrace for our picnic. On warm days, the Professor and Root would play catch on the lawn in front of the hospital, and then we'd have tea and talk some more. The bus home was just before two o'clock.

Often the widow was there as well. She would usually leave us alone with the Professor and go off to do some shopping for him, but sometimes she joined in our conversation and even brought out sweets to have with our tea. She had settled quietly into her role as the one person on earth who shared the Professor's memories.

These visits continued for some years, until the Professor's death. Root played baseball—always second base—through middle school and high school, and in college, until he injured his knee and had to give it up. And I worked as a housekeeper for the Akebono Housekeeping Agency. During all those years, even after Root was old enough to grow a mustache, in the Professor's eyes he remained a small boy in need of protection. And when the Professor could no longer reach high enough, Root would bend over so the Professor could rub his head.

The Professor's suit never changed. The notes, however, having lost their usefulness, fell off one by one. The one I had rewritten and replaced so many times, the one that read "My memory lasts only eighty minutes," disappeared eventually; and the portrait of me with the square root sign faded and crumbled away.

In their place, the Professor wore a new decoration: the Enatsu card we had given him. The widow had made a hole in the plastic sleeve and run a cord through it, so the Professor could have it hanging around his neck.

Root never came to visit without the glove the Professor had given him. And if their games of catch were less than brisk, they could not have enjoyed them more. Root tossed the ball gently for the Professor, and no matter where the return went, Root did his best to run it down. The widow and I would sit on the lawn nearby. Even after Root's hands had grown and the glove no longer fit, he continued to use it, claiming that a tight glove was good for a second baseman since it allowed him to handle the ball quickly and send it on its way to first. The leather faded and the edges frayed, and the label had long since torn off. But you had only to slip your hand inside it to feel the shape of Root's palm worn into the glove.

Our last visit to the Professor was in the autumn of the year Root turned twenty-two.

"Did you know that you can divide all the prime numbers greater than 2 into two groups?" He was sitting in a sunny spot, pencil in hand. There was no one else in the lounge and the people who passed by the door from time to time seemed far away. We listened carefully to the Professor. "If n is a natural number, then any prime can be expressed as either $4n + 1$ or $4n - 1$. It's always one or the other."

"All of those numbers, those infinite primes, can all be divided into two groups?"

"Take 13, for example . . ."

"That would be $4 \times 3 + 1$," Root said.

"That's right. And 19?"

"$4 \times 5 - 1$."

"Exactly!" The Professor nodded. "And there's more to it: the numbers in the first group can always be expressed as the sum of two squares, but those in the second can never be."

"So, $13 = 2^2 + 3^2$."

"Precisely!" said the Professor. His joy had little to do with the difficulty of the problem. Simple or hard, the pleasure was in sharing it with us.

"Root passed the qualifying exam to become a middle school teacher. Next spring, he'll begin teaching mathematics." I could hardly contain my pride as I made my announcement. The Professor sat up to hug Root, but his arms were frail and trembling. Root bent down to embrace him, the Enatsu card hanging between them.

The sky is dark, the spectators and the scoreboard are in shadow. Enatsu stands alone on the mound under the stadium lights. The windup. The pitch. Beneath the visor of his cap, his eyes follow the ball, willing it over the plate and into the catcher's mitt. It is the fastest one he has ever thrown. And I can just see the number on the back of his pin-striped uniform. The perfect number 28.

www.vintage-books.co.uk